# BORN RICH, LEARN POOR

## Love Attracts, Fear Repels

Dr. Ming Way

Born Rich, Learn Poor: Love Attracts, Fear Repels
© 2021 Ming Way and 4PM Zen Productions
No portion of this work may be copied, used or stored in any way
on any type of information storage/retrieval system without
the express written permission of the copyright holder.

ISBN: 978-1-953487-00-1 (paperback)
ISBN: 978-1-953487-01-8 (ebook)

Printed in the United States of America
by Three Knolls Publishing & Printing | Tucson, Az
www.3knollspub.com

For my parents who believe that
animals are smarter than humans

# Acknowledgments

I owe a debt of gratitude to some special friends. They are the most sincere, free-spirited, unpretentious fellas I've ever known. Their existence often reminds me that words might be a human invention that clouds the real experience of life.

First of all, I would like to thank a rooster. He strutted and swaggered like a general, bullying the little ones like me. I once attempted to share a steamed bun with him for friendship, but only lost the food and gained a scar on my hand. He traumatized all the toddlers in the village without saying a word. His cocky presence was the first incarnation of Fear in my childhood memories.

A polar opposite that I am particularly grateful to is my childhood feline sweetheart. We slept together during cold winters. Her purring lullabies made me feel joyful and bonded. She loved sharing – mice, sparrows, cicadas, and once, a golden snake. She didn't lecture nor ground her kittens, but she was among the most loving and yet strict mothers I have ever known. The warm and purring ball of fur was the embodiment of Love to a young girl.

I wish to acknowledge Yinu, my coolest canine friend. He was neither a pet nor a guard but a family member with minimal obligations and maximum freedom. While he trotted around the village, playing, courting, and fighting in his own kingdom, he was also extremely compassionate, loyal, respectful, and protective as a family member. He dragged himself across the entire village to die at home one cold winter night. He was the epitome of free will. Freedom and willingness, Yinu was the space between Fear and Love.

And finally, my deepest appreciation goes to Michael David, a bear friend. I would not and could not finish this book without his unwavering encouragement and support. As my business and life partner, MD often amazes me with his paradoxical existence: he is artistic yet managerial, creative yet technical, innocent yet judgmental, sophisticated yet childish, strong-willed yet whiny, highly-sensitive yet loud, sporty yet fluffy, loving yet fearful… he is the unity of the polar opposites, my paradoxical One.

# Contents

Aperitif. . . . . . . . . . . . . . . . . . . . . . . . . . . . . . . . . . . i
The Sanctuary . . . . . . . . . . . . . . . . . . . . . . . . . . . . . . 1
Tai Chi under a Tree . . . . . . . . . . . . . . . . . . . . . . . . . .7
Bedtime Story . . . . . . . . . . . . . . . . . . . . . . . . . . . . . . 13
Death Messenger . . . . . . . . . . . . . . . . . . . . . . . . . . . 19
Magic Trip. . . . . . . . . . . . . . . . . . . . . . . . . . . . . . . . . 25
Origin. . . . . . . . . . . . . . . . . . . . . . . . . . . . . . . . . . . . 29
Life Lab . . . . . . . . . . . . . . . . . . . . . . . . . . . . . . . . . . 33
Love and Fear . . . . . . . . . . . . . . . . . . . . . . . . . . . . . 39
Love and Essence . . . . . . . . . . . . . . . . . . . . . . . . . . 45
The I Resort . . . . . . . . . . . . . . . . . . . . . . . . . . . . . . 53
Love Balloon . . . . . . . . . . . . . . . . . . . . . . . . . . . . . 59
Love Bond . . . . . . . . . . . . . . . . . . . . . . . . . . . . . . . 63
Dog Wobbles, Cat Burns . . . . . . . . . . . . . . . . . . . . 69
Essential Observer . . . . . . . . . . . . . . . . . . . . . . . . 75
Infected Cat . . . . . . . . . . . . . . . . . . . . . . . . . . . . . 81
Lawsuit. . . . . . . . . . . . . . . . . . . . . . . . . . . . . . . . . 85
The F Word . . . . . . . . . . . . . . . . . . . . . . . . . . . . . 91
The D Lair . . . . . . . . . . . . . . . . . . . . . . . . . . . . . . 99
Fear Bubble. . . . . . . . . . . . . . . . . . . . . . . . . . . . 105
Desert Oasis . . . . . . . . . . . . . . . . . . . . . . . . . . . 111
Sighted Blindness . . . . . . . . . . . . . . . . . . . . . . . 117
Infected Dog . . . . . . . . . . . . . . . . . . . . . . . . . . . 121
Lost Cause. . . . . . . . . . . . . . . . . . . . . . . . . . . . . 129
Universal Language. . . . . . . . . . . . . . . . . . . . . . 135
Love Attracts, Fear Repels. . . . . . . . . . . . . . . . . 141
Hyenas' Laugh . . . . . . . . . . . . . . . . . . . . . . . . . 149
Fear Charged . . . . . . . . . . . . . . . . . . . . . . . . . . 155
Shapeshifting. . . . . . . . . . . . . . . . . . . . . . . . . . 163
Barnyard of Commerce . . . . . . . . . . . . . . . . . . 171

Privileged Quarantine . . . . . . . . . . . . . . . . . . . . . 177
In the Cloud. . . . . . . . . . . . . . . . . . . . . . . . . . . . 183
Monster in the Middle . . . . . . . . . . . . . . . . . . . . 187
The Virus Code. . . . . . . . . . . . . . . . . . . . . . . . . . 193

# Aperitif

Somewhere in the Milky Way orbits a blue Planet **F**, an economic superpower in the cosmos. After the extinction of Homo sapiens and then Homo fatuuses, intelligent anthropomorphic animals have dominated the place. Sophisticated artificial intelligence (AI) robots have replaced the lion's share of labor as well as knowledge workers; highly advanced genetic engineering techniques have conquered most animal diseases. If one can afford all the treatments, they will live for-almost-ever.

Nonetheless, a deadly epizootic caused by an unknown Virus is encroaching the **F** society. What baffles the medical experts is that the Virus does not attack any organs, but seems to live off something even more fundamental to intelligent animals. The infected claim that they have lost essential purpose to live on. Symptoms vary from apathy to anger, depression, occupied meaninglessness, gregarious emptiness, and intimate loneliness. Killing oneself or others signifies the final stage of the disease.

Hence, a fast-growing number of the **F** residents seek a way to emigrate to the Sanctuary, a bitterly coveted clean zone in space, free of the Virus and saturated with joy and happiness. There is only one precondition for getting in line: being RICH, as the Sanctuary is a place where only do the rich have access. Among those who strive to get rich and move away is this family.

The family lives in Star Valley, a hidden gem nestled between the Nether Mountains. Tinkling streams slither into the Mirror Lake, nourishing the valley's land and life. Like a beautiful apple that rots from the inside, the small town suffers from all sorts of disturbances and crimes. Beside the high rates of suicide and murder, Star Valley constantly witnesses disputes and fights, alcohol and drug abuse, sexual harassment and assaults, animal trafficking and mass shooting cases. All neighbors emit strong vibes of distrust and hostility.

***********

**Family members:**

Polisco is a polar bear. Everyone calls him Pol. His wife, PanRoo, and his friends facetiously refer him as Police-Co, or simply, Police.

Polisco is a local Fluff (a name that conservative Planet **F** residents proudly call themselves). He attended the prestigious Icyleague Polar University with a double major in computer science and economics. He works at an AI software company in Star Valley and hates his job.

Polisco burps and farts loud and proud. Like many male Fluffs, he glorifies his bulge, balls and beyond. Also, like many Fluffs, he is a fervid sports fan. He is particularly loyal to his alma mater snowball team (a competitive spectator sport in which the players use their paws and claws to pass and throw a big snowball into the rival team's net to score): the Snow Monsters.

Polisco is obsessed with being in control of every aspect of his life. He also judges others in town in a patrolling fashion. When he sees something or someone out of line, he becomes angry and roars. This very behavior cost him a gunshot in the chest during a road rage chase last year. His signature mantra goes like this: "***I am the boss of everything!***"

***********

PanRoo is half-panda-half-kangaroo. She goes by Pan among the family. Polisco affectionately calls her Pansy.

PanRoo is an immigrant from Moon Sticks, one of Planet **F**'s natural satellites. Because Planet **F** sends all its garbage to Moon Sticks, some overly proud Fluffs refer to PanRoo and her moon fellows as Stinkers. A couple of years ago, PanRoo left her motherland for a master's degree in Education on Planet **F**, where she found the love of her life on a dating app for bears.

PanRoo teaches at the only school in Star Valley. Like many lady bears, she cares deeply about proper looks and social etiquette. She also has serious penis envy. Although the cute panda face, together with a kangaroo pouch on her tummy makes her a lovely lady, she wishes she were a powerful, privileged man. To balance her power hunger, PanRoo savors her husband's ultrasensitive nipples against his will and fancifully simulates mounting and humping with her non-cooperative polar bear partner.

PanRoo is extremely sensitive about her accent and strives to assimilate into **F** culture. She ascribes her failure to be elected to the homeowner's association committee to her immigrant background. The slightest hint of disapproval or exclusion from others stresses her out. PanRoo's signature mantra is: ***"It is indeed inappropriate!"***

\*\*\*\*\*\*\*\*\*\*\*

Joecub is Polisco and PanRoo's only cub. The toddler is nicknamed Jo.

Joecub is a happy cub that loves playing and laughing. He is curious, authentic, imaginative, and adventurous. He is currently in the phase of imitating what the adults have to say with his cubbish twist of words.

Unlike his father Polisco, he doesn't make plans, nor does he try to control the results. Thus, he wanders through life freely and spontaneously; unlike his mother PanRoo, Joecub knows nothing about the appropriate ways, so he responds to the world in immediate and natural ways. His vocabulary is limited, but he asks essential questions that the adults are too busy learning and explaining the answers to ask why in the first place. As he grows bigger, and as the adults are eager to show him the how, Joecub often coos his cubbish mantra with a puzzled look: "**but why?**"

Jo has a best friend. His name is BarKockalotte, the companion dog who loves everybody in the family...well, almost everybody.

\*\*\*\*\*\*\*\*\*\*\*

BarKockalotte, the neutered companion dog, likes being addressed as Mr. Bar. Every time Polisco mocks him by calling him "Bark-A-Lot," the dog unfailingly reminds his impish master that the emphasis of his name lays on "Kock," not "Bark."

BarKockalotte is a Canine Police Academy dropout. His previous master was an alcoholic. After his intoxicated ex-master set the house on fire and burned himself to death, the traumatized dog couldn't manage to finish his education. At that point, the family adopted him.

He loves reading as well as crafting his police dog skills. He is erudite, expository, and protective. Emotionally, Mr. Bar has abandonment anxiety and hates alluding to balls of any kind, intentional or innocent, in conversation. He also detests all sorts of addictions.

BarKockalotte worships authority. He holds his masters' words as universal truths. He, too, believes in all sorts of experts, data and statistics. The dog religiously follows the chain of command in the family: the masters, Polisco and PanRoo, are the top commanders, and then Joecub his best friend, and then him. BarKockalotte deems

Purrplexy the cat to be beneath him. However, she is defiant and challenges his authority quite a bit. Thus, the companion dog fights with the cat incessantly. He doesn't have a full mantra expression, but he often starts his woofs and barks with: "*According to*…" for validation.

\*\*\*\*\*\*\*\*\*\*\*

Purrplexy is the feline companion of the family. She prefers being called Lexy because Lexy the cat is damn sexy.

Purrplexy joined the family a year later than BarKockalotte. She used to be in show business. Because the Virus has shaken the entertainment industry so hard, she had to get a day job as a feline companion. Purrplexy's new dream is to become a cyber celebrity on MeowTube (a feline video sharing platform on FNet.)

Purrplexy is a sybaritic cat who is glued to her fPhone. She is also quite addicted to catnip products. Besides her fPhone, fame, drugs and sex, Lexy does not care about much. She sleeps, cleanses, purrs, and gives excellent massages to family members with her soft paws. The cat doesn't get along with the dog because she thinks that he is an ugly brown noser who has no opinions of his own whatsoever, and yet lectures her a lot. The annoying dog also hides her catnip snacks and gives her long speeches on addiction-induced health hazards. Purrplexy often meows or yowls her mantra: "*Leave me alone! I don't care!*"

However, Purrplexy is jealous. She is jealous of LeDrun, the magic tortoise that the family has saved. Not only does the tortoise have magic powers, but he also claims that he knows how to get to the Sanctuary, legendarily the safest, richest, and happiest place in the universe.

\*\*\*\*\*\*\*\*\*\*\*

LeDrun is a mysterious tortoise with magic powers. Because he drinks a lot through a crystal flask, Polisco half-jokingly calls him LeDrunk, among many other offensive nicknames he has coined for the tortoise.

Nobody knows much about this tortoise. This past Good Friday morning, he appeared on the family's backyard lawn, covered with blood, seemingly dead. PanRoo put him in her pouch in attempt to revive him. Somehow, it worked. During his recuperation, the tortoise has decided to stay with the family to help them beat the Virus.

LeDrun loves meditating on the family's bay windowsill in the sunroom and practicing Tai Chi under a large maple tree in the backyard. He chants in a way that sounds profound, but also senseless. He barely moves, but he seems to know everything happening around him. Strange indeed.

LeDrun mumbles lots of obscure chants at an obnoxiously slow speed, which bores the family to death. However, it is just a minor flaw to put up with when considering the benefits of his magic powers, such as taking the family to magic story adventures or turning them into something else.

As a borderline abuse of magic power, LeDrun plays all sorts of pranks on the family along their mystical journey to the Sanctuary.

# 1

# The Sanctuary

Polisco comes home from work. He kicks off his round leather shoes and throws his black work bag on the floor. The polar bear then picks a wedgie, scratches an itch down there, and sniffs his middle and ring paw fingers making a quasi-rock and roll gesture.

PanRoo is watching FNet TV on the couch in the living room. Polisco sneaks behind the couch and then stands on his tiptoes in an attempt to tap PanRoo with his member on the back of her fluffy black and white panda bear head.

"Don't even think about it," warns Pan, pausing the TV.

"I don't know what you're talking about," denies Pol, retracting the weapon.

"I just wanna give you a kiss." Polisco holds PanRoo's chubby cheeks with both paws from behind the couch, bends over, and kisses her on the forehead.

"Eww, where did you put your paws just now, Stench Ball?" the panda kangaroo puckers up her round face.

"I miss you too," beams the polar bear. He puts his stubby index finger in his right nostril and launches a spelunking expedition.

"I witnessed another road rage shooting on my way home today," reports Polisco.

"They exchanged fire from inside their self-driving cars for like twenty minutes before the cops started chasing them. It practically gave me chest pains," narrates Pol, reliving his own dark experience of getting shot in the chest in a road rage chase last year.

"Agh! Tell me something new," frowns PanRoo.

"Our porcupine neighbors across the street got all their cars bulletproofed. Do you want to armor our vehicles too? I follow local and global news: the number of Virus-caused deaths increases exponentially every day. Our fellow animals of Planet **F** either end up killing themselves or being killed. We need to get rich and move to the Sanctuary for good. This planet is doomed." Pan rests her head upon the back cushion and looks up at Pol's fuzzy double chin.

A small flake of Polisco's booger swirls down and lands safely on Pan's furry forehead.

"Trust me. I dream about the Sanctuary every night. But the Sanctuary is not for the middle-class. We don't even have the budget for bulletproofing our cars. We don't even have ventilated car seats. That's why you smell what you smell. Anyway. Enough about my smegma. How was your day, Pansy?" teases Pol, dabbing the tip of Pan's black nose with his booger finger affectionately.

"I knew it was your fumunda cheese!" Pan slightly tilts her head and snuffles. "My day? Working from home with a toddler and three pets is such a nightmare! And for the last time, stop calling me Pansy!"

"Oh! I cannot call you Pansy, but you can call me Stench Ball? I think my paws smell like heaven. Sniff again," boasts Pol, forcefully covering Pan's nose with his giant bear paw.

"Knock it off! It's time for ventilated car seats!" Pan raises her voice and pushes away the intruding paw.

"You're right. The damn car seat gives me EBS... excessive butt sweat, you know. Speaking of EBS, is that why you're wearing a short sundress? Or are you expecting someone? Better be a woman," grunts the territorial polar bear.

"Relax," smiles Pan while shaking her head. "It's Pilferine, our raccoon neighbor from next door. She told me on the phone that she would stop by and explain to us the new front yard sanitary regulations from the homeowner's association. She said we should unite together as a community to fight against the Virus."

"Oh! You're dressed up for that busybody?" laughs Polisco with contempt, "I am sure that's how we glue together as a community. More regulations!"

"It's inappropriate to greet our neighbor in PJs. Plus, Pilferine's husband killed himself just a couple of months ago. Don't be rude to her," says Pan, tidying up her black and white polka dot dress.

"I would've killed myself too if I had to live with her!" growls Pol.

"Indeed inappropriate!" screeches Pan.

"Fine. You are so nice and proper, but why did they vote you down for being elected to the HOA committee?" Polisco provokes PanRoo.

"How dare you? You know exactly why. It's because I am an immigrant, a Stinker from a moon of Planet **F**. Of course, I don't deserve the privileged HOA seat," mutters PanRoo, face dimming down.

"You think that's a privilege? I am telling ya. HOA is the worst thing that ever happened to this community. But don't worry, Pansy. I have an idea!" sneers Pol.

"Knowing you, it's probably something related to poop or pee," mocks Pan, raising her arms backward to scratch Pol's furry potbelly.

"Hey! Life is all about the moments on the shitter!" Pol imparts his life wisdom.

"I've installed a motion-sensor sprinkler system for our front lawn. Any trespassers of an unsafe social distancing radius will be greeted with Pol's royal golden showers!" the impish polar bear smirks with anticipation.

"Don't tell me you peed in that big tank you recently attached to our sprinkler system. You are so not going to do that, Police-Co!" yells Pan, genuinely concerned.

"What? You won't let me do anything fun! By the way, I bet you a bucket of gold that the raccoon neighbor doesn't show up," predicts Pol.

He holds Pan's paws off his belly and up in the air to keep them off his fat part.

"Why not?" asks Pan with palms together above her head as if she were in a seated yoga pose.

"Because Pilferine is a fraud! Her words and actions never match! She can bullshit about community caring all she wants, but I know she is the one who leaves her trashcans outside after pickup day! Remember her overgrown lawn and untrimmed trees that blocked our driveway? She never picks up her dog's shit on our lawn and lets him bark for hours without shutting him up! And then there's her loud-as-hell leaf blower every Saturday morning!" Polisco patrols and vents about his inconsiderate neighbor.

"You are right. Why don't you write her a ticket, officer?" Pan teases the polar bear.

"I would if I could! And I bet you a bucket of gold that she doesn't show up because she is a fake. She bullshits herself and bullshits others," Polisco opines and judges.

"Stop patrolling everyone," the annoyed panda kangaroo unpauses the TV as closure of the conversation.

"But I am the boss of everything! Where is everybody?" Pol looks around.

"In the backyard playing," replies Pan with her eyes on the TV screen.

# 2

## Tai Chi under a Tree

Polisco pours himself a glass of wine and saunters into the sunroom. Through the big open windows, he can see and hear everything happening in the backyard. He takes a seat in a black leather swivel chair by the bay window, crossing his stubby legs upon the windowsill. Outside the window in the backyard, Joecub the toddler, BarKockalotte the dog, Purrplexy the cat, and LeDrun the tortoise are all playing on the grass under an enormous maple tree.

"LeDrun," woofs BarKockalotte at the meditating tortoise. "I have read everything the experts have to say about the Sanctuay. According to them, the Sanctuary is not only Virus-free, but also filled with love and joy. You always brag about your magic powers after a couple of drinks. Why don't you take us there for good, please? I am so fed up with this place!" whines the dog, splooting on the grass.

"Fat up!" squeals Joecub the toddler, somersaulting next to BarKockalotte.

The cub is in the phase of language imitation spiced up with his own creation.

"You are fed up?" meows Purrplexy by the pool.

"Try reading my MeowTube channel comments. The cyberbullying is so cruel and disgusting that it will literally crush your will to live!" The cat licks her paw and cleanses her face.

"That is because you always post some borderline pornographic garbage on your channel to solicit cheap attention," critiques BarKockalotte and continues, "which is exactly why I am fed up with this place. There are neither morals nor ethics in our society anymore. Everyone is like 'Look at Me! Me! Me!' while stomping on others' toes and ignoring the 'Ouch! Ouch! Ouch!' Then they go at each other in a vicious circle. Yesterday, our porcupine neighbors across the street had band practice in their garage and left the garage door open. Their music was horrific and very loud. And they all stunk of gunsmoke and drugs. I could just smell it. So, I went over and barked at those inconsiderate degenerates. Guess what?" barks BarKockalotte.

"I don't really care," yawns Purrplexy the cat. "But you know those porcupines have got bulletproof cars for a reason, right?"

"The drummer threw his huge quill drumsticks at me," barks the dog, ignoring the cat. "It all happened so fast that I couldn't manage to dodge. One of the barbed quills hit my forehead and lodged in there. Do you know how hard it was to have it removed? Ouch!" BarKockalotte lowers his head to show everyone the wound.

"Why did you have to remove it? You could pass for a dog unicorn with that quill on your forehead," teases Purrplexy.

"You are truly a heartless cat," whimpers the dog.

"Ahh, the Sanctuary," LeDrun the ancient tortoise slowly opens his eyes among the clamor. "**Don't pursue the way to the Sanctuary. Return to it. The more you want to define it, the less you will understand it**..." chants LeDrun.

"But I do want to understand it, aa-ww-ooooooo!" howls BarKockalotte, chin skyward.

"There must be a way to get there. Show it to me. Guide me! I will do whatever it takes! I don't care how hard I have to work! When I was in the Police Academy, I was known for my doggedness!" claims the dog. He begins running around the maple tree to show off his speed and determination.

"Stop running, please. You make me dizzy," grumbles LeDrun, falling on his back and waving his four legs up at the sapphire sky.

"LeDrun die!" squeals Joecub, crawling over to check on the struggling tortoise.

"He's not dead, buddy. LeDrun will take us to the safe and happy place together," woofs the dog as he stops running, using his paw to help LeDrun flip over.

"There is no safe place out there. It is in here," says the disoriented tortoise, pointing his claw at his chest.

"Without interference. No coercion. Like this maple tree. **We are all born rich**," articulates LeDrun, squinting his eyes as he looks into the beams of sunlight coming through the maple leaves.

"No. I'm not! I'm just a proletariat dog. Do you think master Pol and Pan are rich? What are you looking at?" BarKockalotte looks into the leaves and beams, where LeDrun gazes.

"Right," laughs Purrplexy. "They are still sitting on their middle-class asses in this infected small town."

"Mid-ass--" Joecub pouts his lips out, twisting Purrplexy's words.

"How dare you talk about our masters like that!" The dog snarls at the cat.

"The Sanctuary cultivates your indefinite potential. Being rich is the essential vehicle through which you venture a journey to reach the realm. Now, if you will excuse me, I feel like playing some Tai Chi," rumbles LeDrun.

"There must be a way to follow. Your words are so elusive." The dog rests his head on his front paws and gives the tortoise a side-eye.

"Don't be a follower," smiles LeDrun.

The ancient tortoise slowly stands up on his hind legs.

"Count me in! I need to burn some calories!" meows Purrplexy. She jumps behind the standing tortoise.

"I also want to play!" BarKockalotte lines up behind the cat.

"Me two!" Jo the cub joins the party.

"Fine. But be quiet. Now stand flat on your feet and close your eyes," LeDrun starts instructing. "Hold both your front paws at your bellybutton. Remember, the bellybutton is the origin where all movements emerge and return. Now palms down. Clear your mind. Take a deep breath."

Polisco, watching from the sunroom, is amused by the lined-up Tai Chi scene as well as intrigued by the Sanctuary conversation.

"Slowly raise your paws from your bellybutton to your eyes and start parting your paws to different sides to draw a huge ball. Imagine that you are inside the ball." LeDrun is playing with concentration and elegance. "And once your paws meet at your bellybutton from both sides, raise your right paw to..."

"Ouch! I stepped on a pebble!" BarKockalotte exclaims in pain.

"That's enough for today!" shouts LeDrun, ending the session abruptly.

"Wait! Are you upset at me? But I am hurt!" moans the dog, following LeDrun and limping into the sunroom.

\*\*\*\*\*\*\*\*\*\*\*

"Master Pol, I am so glad you are home! How was your day? Do you want to play?" hurrahs BarKockalotte with exhilaration at the sight of Polisco in the sunroom. He plunges into Polisco's arms, hugging and licking his face with a big smile.

"Hey! Nice to see you too, 'Bark-A-Lot'!" Polisco mispronounces the dog's name playfully.

"Master Pol, for the last time, it's Bar-Kock-a-lotte! The emphasis lies on 'Kock'!" The predictable dog objects and explains the correct pronunciation as always.

While Polisco successfully tricks Mr. Bar into saying the word, LeDrun speeds up to pass them in the fast lane.

"Hey! LeDrunk!" Polisco greets LeDrun while pressing his massive bear paw down onto the tortoise's shell to stop him.

"You know the being rich crap you said out there? We are going to reach the Sanctuary before these other lunatics and slackers in town, right?" Polisco fishes for the answer he wants to hear.

"You are **discovering**, not **comparing**. Now, if you could remove your gigantic bear paw from my shell, please. I cannot breathe," pleads LeDrun in a suffocated voice.

"My BALLS are comparing," mumbles the polar bear. "At least I am better than the raccoon bullshitter next door," grunts Polisco with disappointment, lifting his paw.

"Nope!" LeDrun shakes his head, taking a deep breath and marching away.

Head hanging down, Polisco returns to the living room. At the sight of PanRoo in pajamas, he immediately feels uplifted.

"Ok. Pansy, where is my bucket of gold?" The polar bear grins cheerfully.

"Shh! I am watching the Woo-Woo Report on TV here. I just love the supernatural world! Anyway, it is speculated that a death messenger is missing. I have a hunch that LeDrun..." whispers PanRoo in a muffled and terrified voice.

"Don't!" LeDrun's low, hoarse voice resonates through the air, but the tortoise is nowhere in sight.

# 3

## Bedtime Story

It begins drizzling outside. Raindrops knuckle maple tree leaves, making them giggle and blush. Two blue jays in the tree shut their big mouths, concentrating instead on finding a better spot to perch. In the sunroom, Joecub and BarKockalotte are playing fetch while Purrplexy is recording herself. PanRoo starts cooking dinner in the kitchen. She is making scallop dumplings with squid ink wraps. Polisco saunters into the kitchen and slouches against the wall.

"What are those on the cutting board? Are they lumps of coal?" assumes Polisco, the easy target.

"Those are squid ink doughs. My paws got all black, thanks to the ink. And why would I put coal on a cutting board?" PanRoo gives her husband an intelligently superior grin.

"But your paws ARE black, my panda bear!" Pol marches into the kitchen and squeezes Pan's butt while passing her.

"Someday, when we are rich, I will buy you a robot chef. You just press the button, and it'll cook you any cuisine you want!" Polisco leans against the counter and starts poking the black doughs with his fat finger.

"Right," Pan rolls her eyes. "How do we get rich exactly? On my teacher's salary or your student loans? If we ever get rich somehow, I don't need any robots. I'd rather just flee this plagued planet!" PanRoo shakes her head.

"Don't be a pessimist, Pansy. I have something rich for ya!" claims Polisco.

The polar bear picks up two round clumps of dough and places them under his crotch, chanting:

"My balls! My balls!"

"Shush, Mr. Bar could hear that!" says PanRoo in a hushed tone, pointing in the sunroom direction.

"I've got an idea. Why don't you get yourself a carrot so you can portray the snowman in that movie?" smirks Pan, staring at the two squid ink dough balls in Pol's crotch.

"That's why I married you!" acclaims Polisco.

He opens the fridge and bends over in search of a carrot in the bottom drawer.

PanRoo seizes this golden opportunity of Pol's "face-down-ass-up" position. She rushes behind him, grabs the back of his collar with both her paws and starts humping.

From this compromised position, Polisco can only look down at his crotch and watch as the two dough balls fall and smash onto the floor, flattening into two black pancakes.

"Ou-ouch!" Polisco and LeDrun scream in stereo.

"Oops! Sorry! I forgot LeDrun is still in my pouch," PanRoo pauses her passionate dry humping. She takes LeDrun out of her pouch and places him on the countertop.

"Pan, please! Get yourself a strap-on or something to that effect! I am not shaped properly for this kind of mission. And I genuinely don't enjoy these accidental intimacies with Pol's rear end. Ouch…my hip hurts… I need a drink…" grumbles and groans the ancient tortoise.

"Hold on a second," grunts PanRoo.

The panda kangaroo seems to recall something. She scuttles towards the master bedroom and hops back with a crystal flask in her paw.

"Where did you get this?! I've been looking for it!" screeches LeDrun, exhilarated by the sight of the flask.

"Mr. Bar found it in the backyard the other day. I put it in my jewelry box and simply forgot about it," explains PanRoo, handing it back to the tortoise.

LeDrun holds the flask dearly to his chest. He then removes the cap, presses his nose against the orifice and inhales deeply. A smile emerges on his wrinkly face from the bottom of his heart, like a flower blooming in the sun.

"All shall return," murmurs the mystical tortoise.

"Police-Co, could you tell Jo a bedtime story tonight? I am pretty tired today," asks PanRoo, picking up the black pancakes from the floor.

"One thing, though: no snowball game stories. The last time you told one, he was up all night, kicking and yelling," complains PanRoo.

"Why not? He is almost two years old! It's time for him to bask in the glory of snowball sports," extols Pol, arms open, legs squeezed together, chin lifted, eyes closed.

"Not at night!" Pan passes the polar bear and pokes his potbelly with her index finger.

"Hey! Don't touch my fat part!" growls the chubby polar bear.

"I refuse to tell my son puny, cheesy stories. And speaking of puny,

Bulbous Head, could you tell Jo a story? Maybe a story about the Sanctuary or why you sleep in my wife's pouch? Ouw! Who punched my nuts?" groans Polisco, bending over in pain.

"Sure," burps LeDrun, taking another sip from the crystal flask. "It is time for you guys to know the truth."

"What truth?" The bear couple raise their brows.

**********

When Joecub goes to sleep, he always enjoys bedtime stories. After brushing his teeth and combing his fur, he snuggles up with Mr. Bar, his best friend, and awaits another great story.

"Knock, knock," grunts the mother bear at the door.

Polisco leans against the wall next to her.

"Who's there?" howls BarKockalotte through the door.

"Pan and Pol!" shrills LeDrun in a scratchy voice, sticking his head out of Pan's pouch.

"Pan Pol who?" squeals Joecub with a big smile.

"Pan Pol rule the family and you little poo!" teases the father bear against the wall.

"Brahahaa!" guffaws Joecub. He has recently discovered the entertainment value of the words "poop," "pee," and beyond.

Like father, like son.

BarKockalotte opens the door.

"Master Pan, is the story tonight about family rules? I'd love that! Let me fetch Purrplexy. She needs to hear that!" woofs the dog, dashing out to the sunroom where the feline castle erects.

PanRoo sits in bed and leans against the headboard. LeDrun rests his head on the edge of Pan's pouch and dangles his arms. The cub lies next to his mother's thigh, rolling around and playing with his toes.

Polisco slouches on a large brown beanbag next to the bed. BarKockalotte rushes in, scuffing Purrplexy with his mouth.

The daggling and squirming cat yowls: "Leave me alone! I don't care! Rules are for fools!"

BarKockalotte throws the abducted cat onto Jo's bed and then jumps next to Polisco's feet, sitting up with a big tongue-hanging smile.

"We are all ears, Wenis Head. What truth do you want to announce?" asks Polisco from the beanbag, stretching his stubby legs and patting his bouncy belly.

"Are you like, in fact, a thousand years old? You know I normally don't talk to old fuc…" meows Purrplexy, rolling on her back, stretching her body to reach the tortoise with her front paws.

"Not old. Seasoned and wise. Be appropriate, kitten," PanRoo interrupts the uncouth cat.

"Why—s-s-s," coos Joecub, prolonging the "s" sound like a burning firework fuse.

"It's about the missing death messenger on the Woo Woo Report earlier today, isn't it?" suspects PanRoo intuitively. She takes the tortoise out of her pouch and gently places him on a soft blanket.

LeDrun sits up, crosses his legs, and sighs deeply. He then conjures the crystal flask out of his shell and takes a sip.

"Yes," replies the tortoise. "I am the missing death messenger."

# 4

## Death Messenger

"Aaaah---" the gobsmacked family growls, roars, barks, and yowls. PanRoo grabs the cub and cat off the bed to join the scared polar bear and dog behind the brown beanbag.

"No need to panic. I am not here to take your lives," LeDrun takes another sip and continues. "As I recover from the trauma, my memories and magic powers are slowly coming back to me. I remember that my boss, Death, has many messengers. I am one of them. We work with all sorts of death: murder, accidents, natural causes, legal executions, natural disasters, war, massacres, suicides...and epizootics."

"Including the Virus on Planet **F**," reckons Polisco, peeking out from behind the beanbag.

"What exactly do death messengers do? Do you just show up and tell the poor fellows that their time is up? What about our time? Do you know it in advance?" inquires PanRoo, holding Joecub tightly.

"You don't see us, but we are everywhere," replies LeDrun. "Death messengers have special receptors for receiving the death signals sent by living beings in the universe. Upon receipt, we decipher the information contained in the signals and locate the death sites. We then use the Death Portal to arrive at the site, extract the life Essence from the body, confirm the death, return the Essence to the Origin, and move on."

The death messenger slowly stands up. At the center of his chest elevates a half-black-half-white, round-button-like thingy.

"This is the receptor," reveals LeDrun, pointing at his chest.

"Belly butt!" coos Joecub, resting his chin on top of the beanbag.

"It's not a belly button if it's not on the belly," woofs BarKockalotte. "It's a chest button, to be precise."

"So it's a nipple. Is it sensitive too?" growls the empathetic polar bear.

"Quiet," LeDrun gives the silly animals an irritated look. He retracts the death signal receptor and says: "I know this button is more than a receptor, but I cannot remember. But I do recall that one night I showed up at Pilferine's house."

"Oh! It was Pilferine's husband. He put a r-e-v-o-l-v-e-r in his mouth," barks BarKockalotte the puzzle solver.

"And the following morning," continues BarKockalotte, "Joecub and I came out to the backyard to play, but only found you lying 'dead' under the maple tree, covered with blood. You were so battered that I didn't think you could make it. It's master Pan's pouch that healed you." The dog wags his tail at PanRoo.

"My grandma used to say that our pouches could heal everything," says the panda kangaroo proudly while standing up behind the beanbag. She places Joecub on the beanbag for a rest.

"Ever-th-iii!" squeals and smiles Joecub from atop the beanbag, clueless about what is happening.

"Yeah," frowns LeDrun. "I don't remember what happened to me that night. There is a memory void between arriving at Pilferine's house and waking up in PanRoo's pouch."

"Maybe what happened to you that night was so traumatizing that your brain refuses to remember it," analyzes PanRoo.

"I bet it's our lovely neighbor Pilferine!" speculates Polisco. "I catch her throwing shit over the fence into our backyard all the time: dead flowers, twigs and debris, anything loose in her backyard. I bet she found a 'dead' tortoise in the house and threw him over the fence. It's a force of habit." The polar bear concludes the case.

"It does sound like her," howls BarKockalotte in agreement.

"What happened to being 'invisible' as a death messenger?" questions Purrplexy.

"To be honest, I have no clue. I've never had to show my physical form in the past," LeDrun wonders.

"So, what do you plan to do next? You're still healing." PanRoo worries that she will lose the tortoise forever.

"I'm not going anywhere," assures LeDrun. "You saved my life. I am going to save yours."

"Are you taking us to the Sanctuary?" asks Polisco with sparks in his eyes.

"Eventually yes," says LeDrun. "We will have to fight against the Virus first."

"Why? Let's just leave!" urges Purrplexy.

"It's too late," reveals LeDrun.

The family is silent.

The whole thing is too scary and bizarre for the fluffy animals.

***********

"But how do we beat the Virus? I can barely fight against the loud and visible porcupine neighbors across the street. The Virus is evil and sneaky," woofs BarKockalotte, touching the bump on his head.

"That is the mystery," says LeDrun with frustration.

"The Virus has to infiltrate and colonize the host animal so that it can replicate and live off the victim's life Energy. However, life Energy is endowed from the Origin and channeled through Love and Fear. At which point does the Virus hack into this natural design? And how? I need to go back to the Origin. That's right! The Origin! How do I get there? The button…the button! Yes! I know what to do. I wonder if it is compromised… Does PaGoo still work there? She is the key…" LeDrun contemplates while murmuring to himself like a crazy tortoise.

"Hello! Nuthead!" Polisco waves his large bear paw to the self-talking death messenger.

"Oh!" LeDrun wakes up. "I need to take all of you to this place. It's a long shot but I cannot think of anything else. Do you trust me?"

"I am in!" Polisco proclaims. He bends forward slightly and puts his bear paw on the beanbag.

"Me too!" Pan tops her paw onto Pol's.

"Three!" Joecub follows suit.

"Are there car safety seats for canine companions?" whimpers the dog, ears flattened, tail between the legs.

"Just do it!" yowls Purrplexy, pressing the dog's paw and hers atop the bears'.

The family gathers around the brown beanbag like a huddle ceremony.

LeDrun feels engulfed by a strange, warm sensation that springs from his chest, flowing up to tingle his nose before pouring into his eyes.

"It's said that Love is watery," weeps the death messenger.

The tortoise's body starts illuminating. He levitates above the family huddled around the beanbag, suddenly diving lower to touch down into a handstand upon the pile of paws.

All the surrounding animals' eyes are wide open, reflecting the illuminated tortoise in their pupils.

"Is that…life energy?" asks Purrplexy the curious cat, trying to catch the beam of light like a boxer air-punching hooks and uppercuts.

"No. It's the death ray," smirks the death messenger from his upside-down position.

"Whoa!---" the whole family disbands and flees from the room in a flash.

The door slams shut.

"Wait! Come back! I am just kidding! Come on!" squeals LeDrun as he floats off after them like a chasing ghost.

He smashes his face into the closed door and falls onto the floor.

"These animals have zero sense of humor," mutters the disoriented tortoise, sitting against the closed door.

# 5

# Magic Trip

LeDrun floats out into the dark living room. The family is hiding behind the sliding glass door of the sunroom. He swirls around the house and then lands on top of the glass coffee table in front of the enormous TV. Like a tortoise-shaped glow-in-the-dark sculpture, the death messenger lights up the living room in a spooky purple tone.

"Come on! I was just joking earlier! Won't do it again!" promises LeDrun.

Silence.

"I have elixir! It tastes like heaven and makes the best wine and catnip drinks like toilet smoothie in your mouth," coaxes and baits the death messenger.

He conjures a crystal flask in his claw and waves it in the direction of the sunroom.

"Really?! Where?!" chatters Purrplexy, sticking her furry head out through the crack of the glass door.

"Meow-ouch!" BarKockalotte scuffs her from behind and drags her back in.

"I can do magic! It's called shapeshifting," cajoles and tempts LeDrun.

He suddenly lights up in a milky white color, shifting into a giant illuminated cub pacifier.

"Mommy!" squeals Joecub with excitement.

The cub crawls towards the living room, followed by his daddy.

"Where do you think you are going?" PanRoo scolds Polisco while retrieving the drooling cub.

"Ok, it is time for The Prestige," LeDrun murmurs.

"I can take you all on an all-dimensional virtual trip. It eclipses time travel because it transcends time and space. I promise it will be like nothing you've experienced!" LeDrun proudly announces.

He opens his arms and raises his head as a silver-blue spotlight casts down upon him from above as if he were an opera singer on stage.

"Experience how?" barks BarKockalotte.

The sunroom door opens ajar. In the crack is a sequence of fluffy round faces and blinking curious eyes.

"You mean like virtual reality adventures? According to a recent study, 56% of the VR users..." Mr. Bar cites data as usual.

"No. It is not virtual reality. It is THE reality." LeDrun interrupts the studious dog.

"Oh! And I can render you invisible or shapeshifted. It's up to you." The magic tortoise sits on the edge of the coffee table, crossed legs dangling.

"Then what are we waiting for? Let's go!" roars Polisco.

The family rushes into the living room. The home is filled with animal clamors and tumults again.

"Are we going back to the past? Let me grab a couple of rolls of toilet paper so we can exchange them for gold! That's how you get rich!" Polisco clicks his tongue while tapping his temple with his finger to highlight his smartness.

"I probably should go change and pack!" reckons PanRoo, checking her pajamas.

"Chill, you two," remarks LeDrun. "Again, this all-dimensional trip transcends time and space. And we can all stay invisible. Now, why don't you all get together and put your paws on my…"

"I have questions!" BarKockalotte raises his paw.

"Based on current advancements in science and technology on Planet **F**, time machines are still a pilot project led by a team of top experts in the Global Space and Time Center. They just failed the 999th launch. How exactly are WE going to do it? Where is the time travel machine? Are there risks? What if we have mechanical problems? What if it catches fire? Do you have a Plan B for us to exit the wormhole, or will we get stuck forever?" BarKockalotte nervously fires off a streak of questions.

"Not everything is about science and technology, you nerd dog," meows Purrplexy. "I'll record this trip and post it on my MeowTube channel. It's gonna go viral! Hey! Where is my fPhone?"

"No phones. And you ought to find answers on your own," instructs LeDrun.

The death messenger then manages to lie on his shell. Again, the black and white round button elevates at the center of his chest. He raises his legs up and moans: "Come on. I'm ready."

"Ewww!" gags Purrplexy. "Show some self-respect, you old perv."

"I mean… you all put your paws on the button, one after another, and close your eyes. Just stay away from my rear end." The wicked death messenger giggles.

"Cockpit dips!" shouts Polisco, putting his bear paw on the tortoise's chest.

"I probably should change into something proper. Oh, well!" PanRoo hesitates and figures, placing her paw on top of Polisco's.

"Wee! Wee!" Joecub cheers and giggles, putting his tiny paw on his mother's.

"Oh, I think I am gonna puke! I need a barf bag! I cannot breathe!" BarKockalotte whimpers.

"Just do it!" yowls Purrplexy, grabbing the dog's trembling paw and presses it onto Jo's.

"Are you ready? Close your eyes. We are about to take off. No peeping Mr. Bar!" LeDrun yells at the dog who is squinting his eyes.

The upside-down tortoise beams in purple while his body enlarges infinitely.

# 6

# Origin

In a blink, everything around them begins melting and fusing. The world becomes indistinguishable. No shapes, no colors, no sounds, no images. They open their eyes inside a greyish sphere of **nothingness**.

"Where are we? When was this? I just blinked my eyes. Why can I not identify anything? Masters! Jo! Are we dead? No…!" howls BarKockalotte in terror.

"We are here. Relax," purrs the cat, poking the dog's butt from behind.

BarKockalotte turns around to get his bearing and sees the family.

"Welcome to the **void of nothing,** the **Origin of everything**!" narrates LeDrun in a raised scratchy voice. "I am your tour guide! Look around ladies and gentlemen: no colors, no shapes, no forms, no words, no names, and no images. All it has is life Essence and Energy that constantly flows around and about."

"What Essence? I see nothing but a ball of goo!" growls Polisco.

"I don't care about Essence or goo. All I know is that I cannot show anything to my fans online. Boo-rr--ing---," meows Purrplexy with a pouty face.

"What spatiotemporal dimension is this sphere parallel to? That of Planet **F**? Is it like Precambrian or Posthomofatuus? It kills me when I don't have references!" barks BarKockalotte.

"***Something is limited to something. Nothing engenders everything***," LeDrun utters words of obscurity.

"Eve-seeing-g-g!" exclaims Joecub, sweeping his chubby arms in both directions like blooming flowers waving around and about.

"So why do you have us here to see nothing?" inquires PanRoo, frowning.

"Oh! That's right. You guys are so distracting," blames LeDrun.

The death messenger levitates in midair and continues: "I meant to show you how Essence and Energy circle around and throughout life and death. I mean, in order to figure out how the Virus attacks, we need to go back to the very beginning of life and trace it little by little until we find the source infection. And this sphere is the **Origin**. It contains no physical forms of life. But this is **where all lives engender, and all lives return**. I used to work in the 'return' zone," pauses LeDrun, the tenured death messenger.

"Wait, quit the crosstalk," meows the perplexed cat.

"What Essence? What Energy? Are you talking about drinks or drugs? Not all drugs stimulate you, you know. Some could make you feel quite flaccid..." Purrplexy meows on and on about her experimental expertise.

"Shush, kitten," LeDrun shakes his head.

"You see. The gooey stuff in the sphere of Origin is called life Essence. All lives engender from Essence. When signaled by the ultimate Fear-charged Energy, death messengers go extract the life Essence out of the creatures' physical forms, and then return it to the sphere of Origin for, leaving the corpses to offer the ultimate Love-charged Energy to the world. It is the CIRCLE," enlightens LeDrun.

The tortoise floats around the family in a circle to envelope the animals with a cloud ring, like a holiday wreath hanging on an invisible door.

"So it is like semen," reckons Polisco, face lit up.

"Eee-wwww!" PanRoo and the pets are grossed out.

"See me! No see me!" giggles the clueless cub, tiny paws covering and uncovering his eyes to play peekaboo.

"No," LeDrun reproves Polisco with a solemn face. "Life Essence is more like the root of your natural abilities and instincts, as well as your unique talents and quirks. In other words, your Essence indicates who you truly are. When you were born, in addition to the Essence endowed from the Origin, you were also filled with restless life Energy. Energy sustains your existence, carries your thoughts and feelings, fuels up your actions, and signals your surroundings. You need Energy to survive and grow, and to communicate with the world through vibrations and resonations. In a nutshell, **Essence is unique whereas Energy is universal**."

The family contemplates in silence.

"I don't think I comprehend what you said at all. Am I supposed to feel that gooey Essence or running Energy in me? Because I don't feel anything," whines BarKockalotte.

"So, the sphere of the Origin is more like Mother Nature's womb that gives birth to everything?" comments PanRoo the mother.

"That's an interesting analogy but..." The death messenger is intrigued.

"Oh! My bear Lord! We are inside a hoo-hoo?" Polisco's head

slightly tilts back. He puckers up his nose and holds his breath as if he smelled some animal stench.

"It's a waste of time, LeDrun," yawns Purrplexy.

"I really don't care about your goo-hoohoo talk. Can we go home now? I need a catnip...nap...catnap!" Purrplexy glances at BarKockalotte.

"Patience is a virtue, kitten. Plus, I want you to meet someone," LeDrun smiles mysteriously.

"Who? Where?" The family turns around their discombobulated heads.

"In this sphere, you don't look and identify. You, instead, perceive and experience. Try to find your inner peace and start feeling your surroundings with all your senses. When your energy vibe can resonate with the natural rhythm of the cosmos, you will see all. So, be quiet. Let's try it." LeDrun teaches.

Silence.

"I feel an itch on my back. I cannot even find a tree trunk to rub it away!" complains Polisco.

"Master Pol, I can scratch your back..." BarKockalotte volunteers, grinning and wagging at Polisco.

"Move, warm," Joecub observes.

"It's PaGoo's feet. We have been standing on her big toe the whole time. Look up," LeDrun reveals the main character of his story as he points upward with his wrinkly claw.

"Ahhhhhh-----HELP!" The gobsmacked animals scream in horror.

# 7

## Life Lab

The family's fluffy faces look up to catch a glimpse of a freakish giant. She is juggling with two crystal flasks in her enormous hands.

"This is PaGoo, one of the life messengers. We work together. Well, we used to," introduces LeDrun the well-connected death messenger.

"Papa—Goo!" squeals Joecub, jutting out his lips to greet the giant life messenger.

"You have a similar flask to the ones she is juggling," observes PanRoo curiously while trying to get her bearings on the giant's big toe.

"She'd better not drop one," woofs BarKockalotte, eyeballs nervously moving with the flasks. "We would be smashed into animal cookies."

"I think she is taking a break from work right now. Stretch time, you know. They say sitting is the new smoking. Anywho, you all stay where you are. I am gonna say hello to my old friend," squeals LeDrun.

He launches up like a tortoise-shaped rocket and pauses suddenly in front of PaGoo's eyes.

"Hello, stranger!" greets LeDrun, giving the life messenger an air-kiss.

"Holy mother f...you scared the shit out of me!" bellows PaGoo like thunder.

"You know my boss would kill me if I dropped these flasks, right?" PaGoo pauses the juggling and shakes the two crystal flasks in her hands at LeDrun.

"Relax. Your boss is Life. Mine is Death. We have the same boss in different modes," remarks LeDrun, playing TaiChi in mid-air.

"OK, Smart Mouth. Where the heck have you been? Rumor has it you are dead! Oh, I missed you so much!" says the life messenger.

"Well, I was dead, technically. And somehow, I was revived. Long story. How are you? Ready to deliver another batch of lives to their peregrinations soon?" inquires LeDrun, landing on PaGoo's nose.

"Just about," smiles PaGoo.

"After I charge up the soon-to-be-born babies with Energy from the elixir in the flasks, they will be all ready to go." PaGoo clicks the two crystal flasks in her hands.

"Super!" acclaims LeDrun. "I need a refill my friend! Like last time, the one in your left hand, the magic PHARE please!" simpers the death messenger, waving his tiny crystal flask in his right claw.

"I knew you wouldn't just stop by to check on me. You know I'm not allowed to share the elixir, really. You are asking for trouble." PaGoo scowls.

"Oh! Come on! It's not your first time. Here! Take this fine jewelry material. It glows purple in the dark," offers the death messenger, handing over a crystal piece to bribe the life messenger.

"On one condition," grumbles PaGoo, accepting the crystal and putting it away.

"Entertain me. You know what to do." PaGoo winks and whistles at

LeDrun.

"Hey! I'm still healing!" protests LeDrun with a pouty face.

"The elixir will heal you fast," cajoles PaGoo, waving the flask in her left hand.

"Be gentle and quick. And don't you ever drop me again!" The tortoise then slowly retracts his bulbous head and limbs back to the shell.

"Relax and enjoy." PaGoo grins while she resumes her juggling.

On her big toe stands the animal family. They all look up with mouths ajar, spectating PaGoo dexterously juggling two crystal flasks and a retracted tortoise.

***********

After a while, the life messenger is satisfied with her stretch break. She puts LeDrun on her shoulder and starts marching.

All of a sudden, the animal family on the giant's big toe feels violent turbulence. They roll around and scream, desperately grasping the toe hair to survive.

The giant enters into a slightly brighter, reddish realm.

The family can discern some blurry, fuzzy baby-like shapes.

"This is the life lab," slurs LeDrun to the family.
"Ah-ah!" The startled animals turn around and see a blushing, sweating, and disoriented tortoise from having been juggled around.

"The life messenger endows these soon-to-be-born babies with diversely mixed life Essence that makes each one a unique and distinctive individual in the world," elucidates LeDrun.

"You see the flasks in PaGoo's hands? She is about to equip them with two magic powers for the life journeys they are about to launch," smiles LeDrun affectionately.

"What two magic pow…" before Polisco could finish his question, a deafening and blinding thunderstorm strikes the entire life lab.

The animals open their eyes after the thunderstorm is over. They see that the crystal flasks in PaGoo's hands are gone. Instead, she is holding two huge, shiny axes and waving them with all her strength.

"What is she doing now?" barks the terrified dog.

"She is making a slight crack on the surface of the Origin so the new lives can be delivered to the world," explains LeDrun as he slowly sticks his head out of the shell.

"Like a baby chick trying to peck the eggshell open?" grunts and figures PanRoo.

"Watch out!" Polisco roars and warns loudly.

With a violent vibration and ear-splitting sound, a brilliant beam of light shines inside the sphere.

The Origin is cracked open.

The family feels a strong gust of wind that pulls them towards the opening. They manage to hold onto the edge tightly to anchor their fluffy bodies. Meanwhile, all sorts of baby creatures pass them and burst out through the crack.

"Wow! It is like the birth of a miniature world!" shouts PanRoo in awe.

"The other day, when LeDrun taught us Tai Chi, he said something about imagining a ball and returning to it. We are in it now!" howls BarKockalotte.

"Forget about the ball! My itchy back is killing me!" roars Polisco, putting his big bear paw on LeDrun's chest and demanding a return home.

# 8

## Love and Fear

In a blink, the family is back in Joecub's room.

Polisco sprints out of the room, hurtles through the living room, then the sunroom, and dashes into the backyard. Before his face smashes onto the big maple tree, the polar bear swiftly turns his back against the trunk and starts rubbing. He slithers up and down like a chubby pole dancer, moaning and groaning with great contentment.

In Joecub's room, BarKockalotte howls: "We are back! We are back! We are back! I was so scared and thrilled the whole time. I think I peed my pantaloons!"

"No panties," Joecub leaks out the confidential information about Mr. Bar.

"It's called a figure of speech, buddy," mutters the dog, covering his crouch with a fluffy blanket.

Polisco returns to Joecub's den and throws himself into the brown beanbag.

"In the future, without my approval, nobody touches my shell during the trips!" yells the tortoise with a stern face.

"Fine, Nip Nanny. Can we go to bed now?" yawns Polisco.

"Not yet. It's reflection time. All action and no reflection make you a nincompoop," teases LeDrun.

"You are poop," grumbles the polar bear.

"Remember the birth moment in the sphere of the Origin?" says LeDrun. "Whenever a life is born, it goes simultaneously on the death list. Life and death are one. Together with the body comes your unique life Essence along with the versatile life Energy. The life Essence is your mark, your signature that makes you novel and distinctive, among others. It also endows you with infinite potential to live a rich life. Your life Energy, on the other hand, is your fuel, your agent and your transformer, with which you survive and grow in connection with the world. It manifests your intrinsic Essence into extrinsic reality. Now, close your eyes and try to reflect on your unique Essence and ever-flowing Energy inside you. Can you feel it?" enlightens and instructs LeDrun, slowly closing his eyes.

Silence.

"I feel something inside," moans and grunts Polisco.

"Really? What is it like, master Pol?" woofs and whimpers Bar-Kockalotte.

"A turd coming," announces the impish polar bear.

The family laughs and ewws.

"This whole Essence and Energy thing is too hazy for me," complains PanRoo. "Before we ever fully understand it, we'll probably already have been victimized by the Virus. Can we just flee? This society is plagued. The Virus is everywhere."

"But you are your society," articulates LeDrun. "Can you flee yourself?"

Silence again.

"What do you guys think PaGoo is? Is she canine? I bet the life messenger is a she-wolf!" howls BarKockalotte with plenty of canine pride.

"Pfft---," Purrplexy blows some contemptible air out of her mouth. "You filthy dogs don't even bury your own shits. I bet she is a lioness! Noble and lofty!"

The dainty feline gazes upward and dreams.

"I don't care WHAT she is. But I am telling ya. She is definitely a female because I could see her bouncing boo..." a hint of smirking leaks out from the corner of Polisco's lips.

"Police-Co!" growls PanRoo at her disturbing husband.

"What?! I saw them when she juggled those flasks and, especially when she was waving those axes." The polar bear mutters and shrugs.

"Boo--boo!" coos Joecub to back up at his daddy.

The family slips into a loud and uncivil debate on the identity of the life messenger PaGoo.

LeDrun chants among the family rumpus:

Nothing but everything

The beginning of all things

Darkness within darkness

The gateway of the manifold mysteries

"What darkness and which gateway? Are you alluding hoo-hoo again?" Polisco connects the dots.

"Hoo-hoo, Daddy, what?" coos Joecub, blinking his innocent, round cub eyes.

"A hoo-hoo is um...umm...a slide," Polisco fobs off the inquisitive cub while leering at the drinking tortoise.

"Pilferine yard!" Joecub squeals, clapping his tiny paws.

"I've been thinking, LeDrun. If you could bring us anywhere in a blink, could we all just touch the button for the ultimate destination of the Sanctuary?" BarKockalotte calculates and reckons.

"That's a brilliant idea, Uggo!" purrs Purrplexy.

PanRoo and Polisco nod their fluffy bear heads.

"Don't be speculative smartasses. Remember: the Sanctuary is a place for the RICH! Ahhhh--hhaaaa--, I am tired. You guys are a lot of work." LeDrun yawns while crawling into PanRoo's pouch.

"I meant to ask you," purrs Purrplexy to LeDrun. "The two magic powers in those crystal flasks in PaGoo's hands, does she give them to everyone before they are born? Do I have them?"

"I paid attention!" BarKockalotte butts in. "LeDrun said it's essential FART for the newborns!" The dog swings his head with pride.

"Eww, what is the essence of fart?" gags Purrplexy.

"It has GOT to be feces," Polisco imparts his wisdom.

"Phare, not fart," LeDrun shakes his bulbous head. "Phare is the beacon, the lighthouse, the essential Guide for you to discover your Essence."

"What is in the other flask in her right hand? There are two of them," wonders PanRoo.

"The other one is the essential Guard," answers LeDrun.

"Everyone has two Magic Powers. They are our natural endowments. They are called Magic Powers because they can give our Energy two different charges for the two fundamental life purposes – to survive and to thrive. To thrive is as much self-discovery as it is self-fulfillment, that is, to discover your intrinsic potentialities, i.e., your Essence, and then to manifest them to the extrinsic world. The extrinsic world is both wondrous and dangerous, hence the two magic powers. While one power sheds inner light on your Essence and charges your Energy to actualize it, the other power patrols your surroundings and charges your Energy to protect you with various weapons on your journey." LeDrun yawns, slowly crawling back into PanRoo's pouch.

The discombobulated animals look at each other with puzzled eyes.

"Oh! By the way, the two magic powers bear different names on Planet **F**," adds the tortoise, sticking his head out of Pan's pouch.

"What are they?" woofs BarKockalotte.

"One is called **Love**. The other is **Fear**. **Love guides**. **Fear guards**," replies the death messenger.

# 9

## Love and Essence

The following morning, the sun emerges above the horizon, striving to push through the clouds. The celestial fireball radiates golden red hues, giving the clouds an inebriated, orgasmic blush. Polisco and PanRoo are canoodling in bed, half-awake. Pan buries her panda head in Pol's furry chest, inhaling deeply.

"Mmm—Milk Duds. Nummy num!" Pan moans with satisfaction, rubbing her round black nose against Pol's nipular area.

"For the last time, woman, they are not Milk Duds! I don't lactate! Stay away from my nipples!" growls the polar bear, shoving his bear paw against Pan's forehead to play a stiff-arm defense.

"Fine. But speaking of genitals, I don't think it's a good idea that you told our cub last night that a hoo hoo is a slide. What if someday he says to Pilferine that he wants to play hoo hoo in her front yard? It would be a disaster. I can just see how Pilferine would broadcast the neighborhood scuttlebutt about us," worries PanRoo.

"Ewww, do you have to mention Pilferine in bed? It's a total turn-off!" grunts Polisco as he ceases the caressing of his beloved. "Fine. You have the talk with him."

"Why me?" protests the panda kangaroo.

"Because you are a teacher. You are good at explaining shit. What would I do? Write him a mobile app game? Genital Crush Saga!" raves Polisco, waving his arm in the air as if he were holding a magic wand that drew a bling-bling rainbow.

"You are terrible!" Pan cracks up. She laughs while rolling back to her side.

"I guess I can give him his very first sex education talk. I feel like a fraud though, because I myself am still baffled about my penis envy. Remember that ball of goo, or what LeDrun calls the 'Origin,' where he took us yesterday? I cannot perceive any gooey Essence nor Energy running through me," Pan grumbles.

"I have a ball of goo for ya," flirts Pol.

He wriggles over to spoon Pan.

"Seriously, I mean, if being a woman is my Essence, why do I waste so much Energy imagining I was a man? Does it make me gay?" Pan rumbles with eyes closed.

"Don't overthink it, Pansy. It's simple. You are a special panda kangaroo. That's your Essence. Then you fell in love with a special polar bear. We do things together with our Energy of Love. Now my Love Energy tells me to do things to you," grins the polar bear with lustful eyes.

"Poppycock," grunts Pan, pushing Pol away.

"Being a colored immigrant woman in this society, I don't feel special in any honorable sense. Do you know how much Energy I have to spend every morning concealing these dark circles around my eyes? And look at my brown ears and brown pouch! I wish I were a polar bear. A man polar bear," mumbles the sulky panda kangaroo.

She then grabs an intimate body lubricant tube from her nightstand and inserts it between her legs as if it were the erected symbol of power.

"Oh? A panda bear tries to conceal her dark circles? You've truly humored me. The color of your fur is your natural beauty, my Pancakes. And, seriously, you don't want a penis." Polisco confiscates the lubricant tube between Pan's legs and throws it on the floor.

"Why not?" Pan's penis-envy persists.

"Because you have no idea how hard it is to carry a huge, heavy sack every day," guffaws Polisco, entertained by his own words.

"Oh! And speaking of color, are we still going to the store today to pick up some paint for our sunroom? I'd love to repaint the walls with light yellow, bright and vibrant!" extols Polisco.

"I love sage green, soothing and sophisticated," vetoes PanRoo.

"Right, as if a color could possess high intelligence. Give me a break. I think sage green is pompous," provokes Pol.

"Yeah? I think light yellow is uriney," rebukes Pan.

"But I love light yellow! I am the boss of everything!" bellows Pol.

"And I love sage green! Urine Boy!" Pan makes a face at the polar bear.

"Light yellow!" "Sage green!" "Light yellow!" "Sage green!" the bedroom squabble flies out the window, hovering and swirling above Star Valley.

*******************

At the breakfast table, PanRoo and Polisco are still enamored with the after-shocks from the paint color argument in bed. PanRoo munches her fried bamboo shoots as loud as a coffee grinder while Polisco slurps his seafood soup like a high-powered dental suction device. BarKockalotte gnaws his breakfast bar, whereas Purrplexy flicks her tongue to enjoy some fat-free milk. Joecub has finished his cub smoothie and sucks on the cub pacifier for pleasure. LeDrun is meditating at the center of the table, engulfed in the amplified animal eating sounds.

"Hey, listen up," says PanRoo after she swallows the last bamboo shoot. "What do you think your Essence is? You know, the gooey stuff from the Origin that makes you YOU."

"I know!" BarKockalotte raises his paw. "My Essence is a dog."

"Right," grunts Polisco. "There are millions of dogs on Planet **F**. What makes you special among all other barking fellas?"

"That's easy," meows Purrplexy. "Among millions of dogs, he is the ugliest."

"Oh! Really?" snarls BarKockalotte at the cat. "What is your Essence then? Vanity?"

"I'm not vain!" yowls Purrplexy. "I'm gonna scratch your hideous face!"

The cat flaunts her manicured claws and threatens the dog.

"Hid face!" Joecub joins the club.

"Quiet!" PanRoo disciplines.

"LeDrun? What is your Essence?" woofs BarKockalotte, seeking help from the death messenger.

He sticks his claw out and attempts to poke the tortoise during meditation.

"Don't ever poke me. I'll freeze your paw off," warns LeDrun, as he slowly opens his eyes.

BarKockalotte whimpers while hiding both paws in his crouch.

"Essence," LeDrun chants:

***What's debatable is not essential***

*What's essential is not debatable*
*Love, the intrinsic Guide*
*Spins and connects*
*Reflects and fulfills*
*One's unique Essence*

"THAT doesn't make any sense," jeers Purrplexy while checking out her newly painted claw nails.

"***Essence encapsulates everything as a mysterious one; Love charges Energy to radiate your unique spectrum of colors***," adds LeDrun, ignoring the meows.

"I agree with Lexy," growls Polisco. "It's pure nonsense."

"But, speaking of colors," Pol glances at Pan. "This morning, we debated the new paint color for our sunroom. What color do you guys love, light yellow or sage green?" the polar bear seeks allies at the table.

"I love royal purple because I am a feline princess," The cat yawns, sticking her tongue out to cleanse some milk around her mouth.

"Royal my arse. Purple is the color of death. And the masters get to make the decisions!" BarKockalotte barks at Purrplexy. He then tilts his dog head and watches PanRoo's face for a second and then observes Polisco's for another. The eternal dilemma for Mr. Bar is to choose sides between the masters. With intense emotional turmoil, BarKockalotte whimpers:

"Maybe we could blend the light-yellow paint with sage green?"

"Seems like a poop color to me," Polisco rejects the dog immediately.

"Babycub," PanRoo turns her attention to the little one. "Do you love light yellow or sage green?"

"Gr-een!" Joecub's face lights up.

"Don't even think about using our cub, you evil woman," growls Polisco.

"You know he tends to repeat the last word of a sentence. Watch this." The dad faces the cub and grunts: "Hey buddy! Do you like sage green or light yellow?"

"Yell-low!" Joecub raises his tiny paws and giggles.

"Oops, busted," smirks Polisco as he shrugs with the bear paw palms out towards PanRoo.

"Fine!" PanRoo puckers up her round black nose. "We then need to vote for the paint color. Right now, it's one vote for light yellow, one vote for sage green, and three invalid ones. LeDrun's vote makes the final decision. The majority wins. It's an ancient Homo sapiens legacy called democracy," suggests the panda kangaroo.

"Demon-can-see!" Joecub struggles with the obsolete, strange word.

"Well, the majority doesn't represent you. They just overpower you," declines the tortoise. He yawns as he slowly crawls towards PanRoo's pouch.

"Where do you think you are going?" Polisco places his big bear paw on the table, barricading the tortoise en route to his haven pouch.

"Let's settle this at the breakfast table," says the pouch owner resolutely. PanRoo then covers her pouch to withhold the consent to accommodate the tortoise.

"Yes, please!" woofs BarKockalotte.

"It's very early in the day! Who takes morning naps anyway?" The dog whimpers and simpers, paws in the crouch.

"Well, I do take beauty naps in the morning..." purrs Purrplexy.

"Nobody asked you!" The bear masters growl in stereo.

BarKockalotte grins brightly at the cat, swinging his body to some imaginary triumphant music.

LeDrun looks at PanRoo's forbidden pouch in despair. "Love also makes one vulnerable," murmurs the death messenger. "All right," acquiesces LeDrun. "I have a place that might help you perceive Essence and Love. You'll experience how Love guides you to discover the uniqueness of your true self, and encourages you to radiate your true colors to the world."

Slowly, the death messenger reaches around his back, conjures a crystal flask from inside his shell, guzzles down till bottom up, and burps out his command:

"Paws on my chest."

# 10

## The I Resort

The family finds themselves standing on a mountaintop. White clouds float above like a cotton fedora hat; a winding river flows across the valley like a golden serpent; rocky cliffs show their teeth to each other like snarling wolves. A giant sequoia tree on the mountaintop erects into the clouds, making the animals look like tiny ants.

"Where is this? I don't like the mountains! I am acrophobic!" barks BarKockalotte.

He lies on his stomach, drags his body to the edge of the precipice, sneaks a swift peek down and backs away immediately, moaning as if he was wounded.

"Ladies and gentlemen, welcome to the legendary 'I Resort'! We life messengers and death messengers come here to reflect upon ourselves and comingle with others," squeals LeDrun the tour guide.

"So Purrplexy is not the only self-obsessed one," mocks PanRoo.

"Haha!" laughs LeDrun. "Yes. 'I' is about the true self, the Essence. And no. You don't discover your Essence without the interplay with others. Therefore, 'I' also stands for 'Interplay.' Bear in mind that in the **I** Resort, everything responds to your Energy, which flows through your thoughts and feelings, actions and communications.

That is to say that things happen as you wish. So, wish wisely," apprises the death messenger.

"Interplay how?" scoffs Purrplexy. "There is nothing in here besides this freakishly ginormous tree. No luxury hotel rooms, no fancy restaurants, no heated swimming pools or spas, no golf course, and not even a coffee shop! What can we wish for? A picnic? Camping? Tree climbing?"

"Haha! Use your imagination if you still have one," laughs LeDrun.

"We are standing outside the lobby of the resort. This sequoia tree is the elevator that takes you to the most miraculous destinations. Each branch, each twig, each leaf, and each root leads to a world of wonder. But today, I have a specific destination for you. It's about Love. Polisco, why don't you push on the tree knot that you are slouching against?" instructs the tortoise.

Polisco turns around and sees a large tree knot on the trunk. Reluctantly, he approaches the knot with extreme caution. He then stretches his left paw out to reach the protruding knot while using the right one to shield his face.

"Relax. It's not a nuke button," LeDrun teases the polar bear.

While the family is laughing, the tree knot smoothly expands into a large, round portal, like an elevator opening its circular door.

"This tree elevator will take us to the Love Terrace for today. Follow me," adjures LeDrun, entering the tree.

PanRoo and Polisco look at each other with hesitation.

"What are you guys waiting for? Let's go spelunking!" whistles Purrplexy, sprinting into the tree portal.

PanRoo holds the cub and follows the cat in, leaving Polisco standing outside with a dog barking and snarling at the dark hole in the mysterious tree.

"Shut up, BarKockalotte!" yells the polar bear.

"But I am scared! It looks like a black hole! It'll suck us in, and we'll disappear for good!" whimpers the dog, tail between his legs.

Polisco bends over with a sigh. He picks the dog up and carries him into the tree elevator.

"My distinguished guests, enjoy the 'I'!" A mysterious low voice echoes across the resort while the round elevator entrance contracts back into a knot.

\*\*\*\*\*\*\*\*\*\*\*

The tree elevator begins to descend. The family feels that they are in a grayish wormhole tunnel.

"So, we are moving down inside a tree? It's nuts! I feel like I'm losing gravity. Nauseated!" whines and groans BarKockalotte on Polisco's shoulder.

"Don't you ever puke on me again!" warns the polar bear.

"Visible and invisible. Colors and Essence. Fly without wings. Swim without fins," rumbles LeDrun.

"Talk without sense, p-ttthhh-pp-uu," Polisco makes a Bronx jeer at the death messenger.

"Ouch! Titty twister!" the genitally victimized polar bear covers his chest with both paws and pitches forward in pain. He leers at the snickering tortoise.

BarKockalotte is shaken off Polisco's shoulder and tumbles down upon the cat.

"Damn it, you stupid dog! Get your hideous butt off me! You ruined my fur style! I am gonna kill you!" Purrplexy yowls while punching BarKockalotte like a feline boxer.

Among the animal clamor, the round door of the tree elevator opens up to a beautiful, fan-shaped terrace. As the family steps out of the elevator and stands on the marble floor, their breath is taken away by the striking view of the canyon below. They realize that the terrace is hanging off the steep cliff, like one of the legendary Hanging Gardens of Babylon. Looking up, they see the giant sequoia tree on the top of the summit. Looking down, they see blue sapphire lakes embedded in the expansive, emerald grass valley. And looking afar, they see thousands of gigantic, beautiful balloons floating around in this grandest of canyons. The balloons are of all sorts and colors, leisurely moving at different paces.

"Hot air balloons? How is anyone supposed to relax in these?" questions Polisco as he finally recovers from the nipular trauma.

"They are not hot air balloons," rectifies LeDrun the tour guide. "These are **Love balloons.** They cast a reality of your Essence, through Love."

"I don't know," meows Purrplexy. "Love balloons sound like a low-budget porn setting to me."

"Be careful what you wish for, kitten," grins LeDrun. "Love reveals your Essence and charges your Energy. Observe attentively where your Love-charged energy takes you."

"What is 'Love energy'? Like a roofie brand or something? That shit is illegal…" remarks Polisco, inspired by Purrplexy's comment on porn.

"Energy is your vitality," explains LeDrun, giving Polisco a side eye.

"It sustains you and animates you in every aspect of your life: working, thinking, talking, entertaining, socializing, flirting… The moment you exhaust all your Energy, you are a dead animal. Trust me,

I know one or two things about death... anywho, Love energy is really Love-charged energy. It is spent on what you love or who you love in life. **And only through the interplay between Love energy is your Essence evinced**," articulates the tortoise.

"I don't understand," pouts PanRoo. "What does 'Love energy' have to do with these balloons? Why are we here?"

"Ah, good question," says LeDrun the tour guide. "You are about to go on a Love balloon journey here at the resort. You see the floating Love balloons? They respond to your Love energy. Specifically, these balloons use your Love energy as their fuel to take you to a manifested reality of your intrinsic Essence."

"So, it's like watching a virtual reality show in a balloon theater?" woofs BarKockalotte with excitement.

"No, it's YOUR show," smiles LeDrun.

"YOU decide what you experience, just like in your life. The balloon plugs into your Love energy and whisks you off to your desired experience. Moreover, the interplay of Love energy generates more energy that recharges the balloon, which will take you to explore a bigger world. The ongoing journey reflects your Essence. Now go find out," encourages LeDrun contently.

"Cool! A lovefest!" applauses PanRoo. "But wait, how exactly do we get on a balloon in the air? We don't have wings like birds, nor can we levitate in the air like you. Do you have a private jet somewhere?"

# 11

## Love Balloon

As PanRoo frets and frowns, something floats onto the terrace and lands right in front of PanRoo--a large bouquet of colorful balloons and a wooden cabin gondola suspended beneath.

Without hesitation, Joecub breaks free from his mother's arms and climbs down onto the marble floor. With unfettered excitement, he toddles toward the balloons with paddling arms and giggling squeals. Meanwhile, the wooden cabin opens its double doors like a loving host opening her arms to the bear cub guest. As soon as Joecub gets inside, the bouquet of balloons ascends into the air.

After making a circle around the shocked family, the Love balloons, carrying the cub in their cabin, fly away like a fledging baby owl, and soon disappear among thousands of other balloons.

"My baby!" screams the mother.

She rushes forward in a vain attempt at chasing Joecub and halts at the edge of the cliff.

"Don't worry, Pan. The cub is safe," reassures LeDrun.

"His Love energy is amazingly strong and vibrant so that the Love balloons receive the signal instantly to come to pick him up. Love connection is natural, spontaneous, and immediate, which is somehow damaged in the adults' world. Thus, I want you all to sit down and close your eyes. When you reach a safe zone, your Love energy will emanate and whisk you off to explore. You are about to fly high," nourishes the tortoise.

"I have no idea what you are talking about. Are you sure we will fly, and not plummet and crash like overripe tomatoes?" doubts BarKockalotte, tail tugged between his legs.

"I am sure," smiles LeDrun. "I am also sure that somewhere in the world, a balloon will receive your Love energy and reciprocate. Once you make the magical connection, it will take you on a Love journey to cast a reality of your Essence."

"So, if I pick a balloon for my liking, my 'Love energy' will send a signal and summon her to me, right?" Polisco makes an air quote.

Pol puts his left arm above his round belly and places his right bear paw under his double chin. After making a quick visual scan of the Love balloons in the air, he begins to shop and critique like a hoity-toity patron in a luxury department store:

"Let me see. Humm...the rainbow-colored parachute one is interesting...well, I try to remain neutral in the planet-wide 'pride' movement. Hey! That black crescent balloon is really cool...but it reminds me of the incessant social problems and debates over the colors of our fur. Plus, it will get hot inside from sheer sun exposure. That green one...Oh! I hate green!" grumbles and mumbles the polar bear.

"No, no, no," LeDrun stops the polar bear. "Love charges your energy from WITHIN, which motivates you to brush out its diverse colors. So never calculate and pick what you love. Just immerse and feel. Feel the things you love to do, places you love to be, and interesting animals you love to spend time with. And above all, feel the life you love to create and the unique individual you love to grow into. When you reach that state, you'll sense the strong Love-charged energy WITHIN. And a Love balloon, somewhere, will receive the signal. She will pick you up and make you fly."

The furry family is still quite discombobulated but remains reticent. They sit on the marble floor and try to immerse themselves in the colorful world around them.

After a good long while, a leaf-shaped, sage green colored Love balloon with a bamboo hut gondola hanging beneath lands quietly by PanRoo. The panda kangaroo senses a long-forgotten yearning inside. She enters the bamboo hut with rekindled passion and courage. The leaf-shaped balloon rises up into the air and flies away, like a huge green exclamation mark capering in the blue sky.

Feeling anxious, BarKockalotte opens his eyes and realizes that everyone is gone, except him and a serene tortoise.

"No! The masters are gone! Even the cat is gone! I don't believe it!" whimpers and whines the distressed dog, stomping and scratching the marble floor with his front paws.

"Whenever I am anxious, I have a strong urge to pee," confesses the dog, cocking his right hind leg to aim.

"Close your eyes, and focus on what's WITHIN," says LeDrun, placing a finger between BarKockalotte's eyebrows to calm him down.

"Remember when you were a puppy? Curious, adventurous, wildly imaginative. There were places you yearned to be, and super dogs you aspired to become." The magic tortoise gently blows a puff at the dog.

BarKockalotte closes his eyes again. Slowly, an elated smile emerges on his doggy face. Meanwhile, a round orange-colored fuzzy Love balloon with a bone-shaped navy-blue doghouse swaying below lands next to the dog. He jumps inside the doghouse with wild glee, and yet dashes out with grave concerns.

"What if I fall from the sky and die a premature death?" moans BarKockalotte. "According to the Journal of Canine Studies, the average age of dogs ranges…"

"Love is a Magic Power. Trust it," enlightens LeDrun.

BarKockalotte observes the death messenger's face for a while, and then turns his head around toward the Love balloon. Looking like a martyr, he walks tall and gets inside the bone-shaped doghouse, and yet again slowly crawls back out in agony.

"Just in case," whines the dog, "if anything tragic happens to me, please take care of the masters for me. Oh! And keep Purrplexy out of trouble. She is prone to addict…"

"You won't die!" yells LeDrun at BarKockalotte.

As LeDrun sees the dog off, he sits at the edge of the garden, and dangles his legs off the cliff. From his shell, the death messenger breaks out a crystal flask, takes a long sip, and exhales with deep contemplation. He then slowly closes his eyes and senses the animals' Energy inside their reciprocating Love balloons.

"Someone is going to get hurt," LeDrun's whisper resounds throughout the resort.

# 12

## Love Bond

PanRoo finds herself on a Love balloon ride hovering and circling in the sky. Looking down from above, she sees bamboo forests and velvet grass dancing in the wind, bay horses galloping under the blue sky, and black nose sheep roaming around like dotted puffy clouds.

"This is the place that appeared in my most memorable dreams." PanRoo is enlivened.

The Love balloon heeds her Energy, and lands softly on the grass.

PanRoo steps out of the bamboo hut gondola. She hears the whispering of the wind and leaves, the chitchatting among the sheep and horses, and the giggling of a creek flowing through the pebbles and water lilies. A white crane stands on one leg in the water, leisurely flapping her wings in the sun.

A strange feeling arises in PanRoo's heart. The panda kangaroo, somehow, feels herself in a way she's never felt before.

"I am like an electric car that has been running on a low battery for years," thinks PanRoo. "This is the first time I have felt plugged in to charge up."

She senses an Energy charge that penetrates her every pore. So invigorating. So encouraging.

"This must be a Love charge." PanRoo smiles, inhaling deeply, eyes closed in the warm sunshine.

PanRoo begins roaming around her dream place. Along the creek, she passes through the bamboo forest. A unique bouquet of fragrances besieges her senses. Juicy bamboo roots and coy mushrooms beckon her from the ground. Dewy bamboo leaves wink at her in the breeze. The creek flows into a glimmering pond, surrounded by white and purple wildflowers along the bank.

"This feels like home, the place I want to settle," ponders PanRoo.

"Plenty of food, and enough water. We'll build a bamboo cabin by the pond. I'll gather bamboo shoots and mushrooms. Pol and the cub can catch fish in the creek. After dinner, we'll drink wine and play mahjong with sheep and horse neighbors. Sheep and horses...I'd like to meet them...wait..." PanRoo turns around and doubles back.

She digs the most succulent bamboo shoots and picks the most delectable mushrooms, and stuffs them into her pouch until it looks like half a watermelon.

PanRoo greets the sheep and horses on the prairie. She opens her pouch and shares all the treasures she has found in the bamboo forest. She makes mushroom wreaths with grass stems for the baby lambs, and straps large bamboo shoots to young foals' foreheads to fashion them into unicorns.

"Love goes beyond myself," reflects PanRoo among jovial neighs and merry meh-meh bleatings.

"I wonder what is out there beyond the horizon," ponders PanRoo, gazing into the wavy divide between the green hills and blue sky.

* * * * * * * * * * *

At the speed of thought, her leaf-shaped, sage green Love balloon picks her up. She ascends into the sky, in awe of nearby craggy mountains and many other Love balloons.

"I, too, want to pass over the mountains." PanRoo aspires.

The Love balloon begins moving in accordance with her thought.

"Wait." PanRoo notices something.

The Love balloon halts.

"That phallic-shaped, light-yellow balloon is annoyingly captivating." PanRoo realizes that her Love-charged energy causes attraction as her sage green Love balloon accelerates toward the yellow one, and suddenly slams on the breaks before they collide.

She peaks out the window of her bamboo hut to observe the light-yellow balloon. Polisco waves and beams at her, from his swinging balloon gondola that's shaped like two adjoined igloos. The polar bear is soaked, and covered with colorful confetti all over his white, matted fur.

"Pansycakes!" greets the exhilarated polar bear.

"You wouldn't believe where my Love balloon took me! It's the snowball games championship! It also has a killer sports bar with hot waitre... anyway! I got to play in the game, AND to perform in the half time show! We are the champions! We are the champions!" sings and dances Polisco.

The impish polar bear then descends the beer bottle down to his crouch. He strokes the bottle with an intense face and sudden obnoxious motions with his arm, as if to spatter PanRoo with some imaginary liquid.

"Here! Take it! Love is about sharing!" raves Pol with a big smile.

"Police-Co! You are so going to pay for that!" roars Pan from the window of her bamboo gondola.

"You don't let me do anything fun!" protests Pol. "How's your Love balloon trip so far?"

"It's a dream come true!" beams PanRoo.

She then vividly narrates her encounters on the Love balloon journey and shares her rediscovered Love energy with Pol.

"Where are you heading now?" asks Pol. "Because I'd love to see the pond in the bamboo forest where you want to settle! I'm gonna check the fish stock in the creek and say hello to the horse and sheep neighbors!" The polar bear neighs and snorts like a lousy imitation of a horse.

"I was about to fly above the mountains to explore before I was attracted to your ugly light-yellow balloon." Pan laughs.

"Same here! I was headed in that direction, and I thought to myself: 'That pompous green balloon is irritatingly appealing.' And bang! My Love balloon just pulled me close to you!" grins Polisco, guzzling and gulping his beer.

"Hey! It's called SAGE green!" squeals PanRoo as she continues, "And yes! I would love to take you to the bamboo forests! But not before you show me the snowball stadium and buy me a drink!" Pan winks and flirts.

"Deal!" exclaims Polisco, tossing the empty beer bottle over his shoulder.

From the flat top of the cliff, LeDrun spots the light-yellow balloon ascending beside the sage green one. Parts of their balloon envelopes appear to be bonded together, and their bamboo hut and snowy igloo-gondolas adjoined. They twirl up in the sky as if waltzing in flight, eventually disappearing among the mountains.

# 13

## Dog Wobbles, Cat Burns

The bear couple flies over mountains and grasslands. All of a sudden, a mirror-like crater lake catches their attention. The sapphire-colored lake is embraced by a handful of snowy mountains. On the lakeshore, a round, orange and fuzzy Love balloon bounces up and down in slow motion.

Responding to their intrigued curiosity, their bonded Love balloons start descending.

Spontaneously, the orange balloon pauses her bouncing as if she knew that she received attention. As a consequence, the bone-shaped doghouse gondola hanging from the balloon stops swinging as it settles on the lakeshore.

From a window near the midpoint of the doghouse, two inflated arms extend out, like two evacuation slides on an airplane. They reach up to the couple's adjoined Love balloons, as if asking for help.

Along the temporarily formed pathways, PanRoo and Polisco slide down toward the doghouse.

The bear couple lands inside a roomy home library. Tons of books on the shelves, together with many police awards on the wall, greet the visitors.

To the left of the library is a home gym that is twice as big as the fitness center back in town.

On the floor between the library and the gym lays BarKockalotte, looking exhausted.

Joecub squats down next to dog.

"Cheers! Mr. Bar!" Joecub shakes the dog's head.

"My sweet cub!" PanRoo picks up the cub from the floor and holds him dearly.

"Hey! Bark-A-Lot! Are you alright?" inquires Polisco.

"Master Pol! I just thought about you," groans BarKockalotte from the floor. "And for the last time, the emphasis is on 'Kock.'"

"What happened? Why is your balloon going up and down like a bouncing testic...orange?" Polisco bites his uncouth tongue.

"I don't know," woofs the dog, struggling to sit up.

"This house has everything I've ever dreamed of! A home library with huge windows, a large fitness center, and have you seen the kitchen? The dog food in the fridge could last for a century! So, I read... I worked out...I devoured. I was wildly happy for a short time. Then I looked out through the library windows and realized I was up in the sky. You know me, master Pol. I have acrophobia. Then I thought: 'I would like to settle down by the lake.' The Love balloon somehow heard me and landed me here like a parachute. I felt safe and content for a while until boredom hit me. When I looked at the fantastic world through the windows, a strong desire for exploration emerged inside me. Then I felt the Love balloon ascend back up into the sky. Guess what?"

"You got scared so you went back to your safe zone?" grunts Polisco, scratching BarKockalotte's neck.

"How do you know that? To my thoughts the balloon responded, and I landed back in this spot," whimpers the dog.

"When security turns into boredom and the desire to explore supersedes, I go up; immediately the fear of heights and the unknown squashes the excitement of adventure. I go down. I've been up and down the whole time before Joecub found me. I feel nothing but exhaustion, like a car running out of gas," sighs BarKockalotte, head hanging low.

"Daddy gas." The cub chimes in.

"Haha!" laughs Polisco. "That's right, cubby! But it's a different type of gas, and I'll tell you the secret recipe: beans, yams, tofu, radishes..."

The polar bear brags on and on about his inexhaustible natural gas reserve.

Suddenly, the family hears horrific screaming from the sky.

***********

The family rushes to the library window to peek outside. A shrilling and howling cat, like a dysfunctional helicopter squeaking its way to a crash site, is falling from the sky. Her fur is on fire from atmospheric friction, which leaves a long smoky trajectory behind her like a falling asteroid.

"I didn't know they had a cat airshow at the resort," barks BarKockalotte.

"That sounds like Purrplexy in heat," discerns PanRoo.

"Purrplexy!" the family comes to a horrendous realization.

As the animals are eager to get out and rescue the cat, another inflatable evacuation slide deploys in response to their Energy. It extends out the window and reaches down to the rocky shore of the lake. As the family slides down to the shore, they see a burning cat diving into the lake with a steamy splash, like a colossal firework failure on a New Year's lakeside celebration.

BarKockalotte and Polisco immediately jump into the lake in search of the crashed cat. While the dog and the polar bear are paddling and circling in the water, LeDrun emerges on the lakeshore, upon his shell is the drenched and charred Purrplexy.

"Oh! My poor kitten!" PanRoo puts down the cub and takes the cat into her arms.

Purrplexy slowly opens her eyes while retching some water from her mouth. "What happened?" meows the cat.

"Let me guess," chuckles LeDrun. "The Love balloon kicked you out in the sky. The balloon launched up like a skyrocket. You plummeted down like a dud firework."

"What? I was almost killed!" coughs and pants Purrplexy, spitting water out like a cat-shaped fountain.

"Wow, what happened to you, Barbecu-cat?" The dripping dog joins in and pokes fun at his feline friend.

"My Love balloon had a killer gondola," narrates Purrplexy, giving BarKockalotte a side-eye. "It was like a royal castle. Everything was so soft and luxurious. Boxes and caves were everywhere. I was resting up inside one of the fanciest boxes, longing for some catnip snacks. Voila! I got an armful of catnip snacks, all the top brands in the world. Then I thought: 'I want to fill up all the boxes with catnip and bring them home!' Bang! Like magic, all boxes and caves were full. Then I wondered: 'If I stuff the entire basket... no!... the entire balloon with catnip treasures, I could open a global chain of catnip castles.' I even came up with a killer brand name: Starnips. The logo would be a feline mermaid wearing nothing but a star-shaped bikini top. And as the founder and CEO of Starnips, Purrplexy would be the richest and the most famous cat on Planet **F**! At that point, I felt a swift falling sensation. But I thought I was falling asleep. You know how sometimes you feel like you're falling in your dreams? Anyway, next thing I knew, I was on the tortoise's shell." The burnt cat regales her tale from the Love balloon journey.

"That's called a hypnic jerk! According to a recent study, 97% of felines have experienced…" reports BarKockalotte.

"You are a jerk! All dogs are jerks!" The clueless cat fights back.

"I am pretty sure you are not asleep nor in a dream, as you were shrilling and howling in your descent, like a mean cat at the vet house," laughs Polisco.

"So, you never even glanced outside the gondola? Oh, my sweet ball of fur! You don't know what you've missed," says PanRoo, patting the drenched cat.

"Why would I?" meows Purrplexy. "I had everything I've ever wanted: luxury, boxes, catnips…and had I not fallen from the sky, I would've loaded the entire balloon with catnips! Do you have any idea how rich I could have become?"

"See? That's the risk I am talking about," barks BarKockalotte. "You fly high. You fall hard. Settling by the lake was not the worst decision, after all." The dog comforts himself.

"But why did the Love balloon kick you out then?" PanRoo is confused.

"Don't forget. LeDrun is the death messenger. I think he plans to kill us one by one. That's why he took us here," Purrplexy presses murder charges against the tortoise.

"Right. I'm sure that's why he dragged your drowned ass out of the water," reproaches Polisco.

LeDrun meditates from upon a big, white boulder among the family hullabaloo. Hearing his name, he slowly opens his eyes and says: "Paws on my chest. Let's take the kitten home to heal."

# 14

## Essential Observer

In a split second, the animal family is back at the breakfast table. Like those who just returned from a most memorable vacation, their bodies are home, but hearts have been left back at the I Resort. After a while, PanRoo remembers to grab a soft towel and wraps Purrplexy up.

"You can pass for a petite burnt dachshund. Small small wiener!" BarKockalotte sings and dances while sticking up his two little fingers in the cat's face.

"Better than none," mumbles Purrplexy.

"Love, the Guide to your Essence," burps LeDrun.

The tortoise then stands up and chants:

**Bright and subtle**

**Strong and delicate**

**Adventurous and vulnerable**

**Spontaneous and persistent**

"Dreamy yet bunk," chatters the burnt cat.

"So, do we get an annual pass or something to the I Resort? Because I would love to play another snowball game with the horses and black nosed sheep!" growls Polisco, eyes sparkling.

"Yes! I miss it already! The creek, grassland, horses and bamboos!" acclaims PanRoo.

"Bam-boobs!" agrees Joecub.

"Another cat airshow would be superb," grins BarKockalotte, tongue hanging out.

"Haha!" laughs LeDrun. "The Love balloon is no more than a magic mirror. It projects your Essence through what you love in life. You all have distinct Essence, hence unique experiences. Your Love balloon trips are self-discovery trips."

"No need for self-discovery," grunts Polisco. "I know who I am, and I'm perfectly clear about what I love in life. Are we done yet? I need to take shower. I stink." The polar bear sniffs his armpits and then puckers up his face.

"Oh yeah?" PanRoo raises her eyebrow. "The Love balloon trip reminded me how much I love country life, but somehow in reality I chose to live in a cookie-cutter home in the city; I've always known that you love music and sports but you don't engage in any activities of that sort except for watching games on TV. I have also known that neither of us are passionate about what we do at work and have always wanted to have our own business...so why have we not made decisions to follow what we love in life? I know we can probably justify every decision. But justification is never a good sign when it comes to Love. How do we discover our potentialities when most of our Energy is spent on things we don't love?"

Silence.

"I'm not sure I follow," whines BarKockalotte.

"Ok," smiles LeDrun slightly. "Do you still remember how you felt when you were meditating in the garden where the Love balloons eventually picked you up? What thoughts or sensations did you behold when your Love balloon appeared? Did you feel energized, vitalized, and fully charged? Were you eager to partake, explore, engage, pursue, or create? That's how Love charges your Energy to take action. On the self-discovery journey, Love is your natural curiosities and imaginations, your instinctive passions and inspirations. As one of the two Magic Powers, Love gives you direction and momentum in making life decisions: by compelling curiosities into explorations, passions into actions, and imaginations into creations."

"Have you considered becoming our nanny? You are hired!" yawns Polisco, pointing at the dozing cub and purring kitten. "I wish Love balloons existed in real life, and not just in your fairy blah."

"Oh, the Love balloons are everywhere in real life. You'll be able to discern them if you heed the Energy flowing inside and around you." LeDrun ignores the mockery and continues:

"In the majestic I Resort, your Love Energy propels the Love balloon, and it, in turn, brings you experiences in accordance with your Essence. In everyday life, everyone has an invisible but palpable Energy field engirdling inside and around the body, waiting to receive Energy charges to power our actions," illuminates the magic tortoise.

"The Energy field, you mean like an aura or something?" ponders PanRoo.

"My balls have an aura," mumbles Polisco, giving the offended dog a quick glance.

"It's got to be blue," sniggers PanRoo.

"Quiet, you two!" scolds LeDrun. "When your Energy field holds a Love charge, it becomes your Love balloon. It will take you to your dreamed experiences. Maybe you find yourself pondering your favorite food or enjoying your favorite vocation with someone, and viola—the experience occurs, and you feel fulfilled. Maybe you are passionate about writing stories, and viola—you become a published author. Maybe you are enthusiastic about a business idea, and viola—your new business takes off. Your Love balloon reveals a cloud of probability of what you desire to experience in accordance with your Essence in real life."

"What cloud of probability? According to quantum physics, the cloud of electrons...hey! I got it! The Essence is to nucleus as the Love balloon is to electrons! I'm a genius! Right?" barks BarKockalotte with intellectual excitement.

"Interesting analogy..." LeDrun is intrigued. "I'm a death messenger, not a physicist. I know that the natural design of life is a complex system that..."

"What about others' Love balloons?" PanRoo interrupts due to her lack of interest in science. "When I saw Pol's hideous yellow balloon above the resort, I felt attracted to it. In fact, our Love balloons flew toward each other and somehow became bonded."

"That's true," confirms Polisco. "Thanks for taking me to the bamboo forests. I had no idea how much joy I could feel from picking mushrooms and playing games with the hoofed neighbors!"

"When your Love balloon motivates you into action, the Love-charged Energy emits Love signals. Your Essence is imbedded in those signals. Somewhere out there, some other animals, not all animals, will receive the signals and resonate with your Essence. They see your potential, appreciate your talents, and are inspired by your intentions or actions. When their Love charges their Energy to **interplay** with you, you see their Love balloons. That's how Love attracts and bonds," articulates LeDrun.

"Nonsense," growls Polisco. "There are no balloons anywhere around me. I miss my phallic Love balloon and its two igloo gondolas!"

"Call it nonsense or whatever you wish. But please respect and trust your own Magic Powers. When you are able to perceive your Love-charged Energy, you will know how to recognize and appreciate others'," replies LeDrun.

"Any signs? Clues? Tips?" frowns PanRoo.

"When your Love balloon attracts and bonds with another, the mutual resonance you both feel is called **joy**," says LeDrun. "More importantly, the ones bonded to you are your **essential observers.** They transform the probabilities into realities. A teacher, for example, could be your essential observer. Through the bonded Love balloons, you realize your music talent, sports potential, or your academic brilliance. Or a friend could be your essential observer. Through the bonded Love balloons, you realize that you are a business genius, a world-class comedian, an inspiring speaker, a terrific consultant, etc. They could be your boss, coworkers or total strangers. Again, your own Love balloon shows you the desired probabilities for *self-discovery*; the bonded Love balloons make them come true for *self-realization*." LeDrun closes his eyes and meditates.

"Wave-particle duality, the observer effect…" BarKockalotte mumbles with happiness.

"There are no Love balloons on this planet," growls Polisco. "Teachers are apathetic; parents are emotionally absent; friends are self-indulgent; coworkers are walking zombies; and my boss is the biggest asshole in the world."

"But Love could also hurt you, or in some cases...burn you..." hints PanRoo while tucking the burnt cat into the towel.

"Nah," LeDrun shakes his bulbous head.

"What hurt the kitten is not Love. It is the Virus," reveals the death messenger, eyes closed.

# 15

## Infected Cat

"Aaaah!" the animals immediately bounce away from Purrplexy, the sleeping and purring cat.

"Is she contagious?" whines BarKockalotte. "She is absolutely offensive, but she is family. I don't want her to die…"

"You'll all be fine. That's why I've decided to stay. We're going to beat the Virus together," assures the death messenger. "But first, let's revisit the incident that happened to the kitten."

"Ok. But why did the Love balloon kick her out? Because she's sick?" inquires PanRoo, going back to her seat at the table.

BarKockalotte seizes the opportunity to wake up the sleeping cat: "Wake up, Charcoal! We all have good news for you! Ouch!"

Purrplexy scratches the dog, half awake.

"Love is natural and spontaneous. It doesn't plan the moves nor try to control the results," elucidates LeDrun. He then opens his eyes, stands up and starts pacing back and forth on the dining table.

"However, Love vis-à-vis control is the eternal struggle of the unwise," continues LeDrun, "also one of the weakest links targeted by the Virus. The journey of self-discovery and self-realization is a dynamic experience between your Love balloon and others'. The 'I' as in Interplay: giving out and taking in, interacting and reflecting, creating and sharing...the moment you attempt to control the natural dynamics, it's not Love anymore. The way of Love is to **generate new, not freeze the old**."

"You are lucky you dove into a lake, and not unto a cactus or something prickly," whistles BarKockalotte, kicking an imaginary ball off the floor.

Polisco sniggers on the word "prickly."

"Hey! I'm the victim here!" yowls Purrplexy.

"So, kitten, when you attempted to control the result, your Energy was not Love-charged anymore. Without the fuel, your Love balloon simply disappeared. All your struggles were inner struggles," enlightens LeDrun.

"I have no struggles, and you have no evidence," pouts Purrplexy.

"It is true that one cannot see your inner Essence nor inner struggles," remarks LeDrun. "But don't forget: PaGoo endows each baby with uniquely mixed Essence, but charges everyone with Love and Fear. Therefore, others around you can perceive the Love charge or Fear charge when you..."

"Snrzzzz, hurrrr, chrguuu, ewborrrrr..." The defiant cat sneers loudly with her multilingual talents.

"I've got an energy booster for ya," barks the dog to the cat. "You have the Virus!"

"I have what?!" screams Purrplexy in disbelief.

"That's my suspicion," sighs LeDron. "Both Love and Fear are natural Magic Powers. They work together harmoniously to make sure we survive and thrive in this life. But what happened to the kitten was not natural: a desired experience has a Love charge whereas a controlled result has a Fear charge. It is absolutely against natural design to use Fear-charged Energy for Love-charged aspirations. It is in fact so **self-destructive** that I have to believe that it's a trick played by the Virus."

***********

"Well," says PanRoo, standing up to conclude the family meeting. "From dreamland to reality, the sunroom has to be SAGE GREEN."

"LIGHT YELLOW! I am going to the store right now!" roars the polar bear.

"Royal purple! I am the princess who lives there!" meows the cat, cleansing her burnt fur.

"A barbecue princess with the Virus?" mocks BarKockalotte.

"***Essence remains a mystery until you paint it out with colors of Love.*** The sunroom is a shared canvas. Paint it with your unique brushes. Let's do it together!" squeals the magic tortoise.

LeDrun stands up on the breakfast table. He floats away towards the sunroom. Along his majestic path, spilling paint cans of various colors to pave a colorful path. The family jumps up and hops out to the sunroom.

The animals splash and smear the spilled paint on the walls, using their petal-like paw palms, fluffy butts and tails, and surreptitious polar bear ball prints.

LeDrun floats up and presses his shell against the wall.

While circling clockwise with his patterned scutum, the magic tortoise chants:

> ***Within, from where Love derives***
> ***Return, that's how Love moves***

# 16

## Lawsuit

A sunny, breezy afternoon witnesses three furry animals and a shelled one in the backyard.

By the sparkling pool, Purrplexy places her yoga mat and starts arching her back for some "cat-cow" stretching. She wears a long, azure silk robe and a merlot chiffon veil. The crimson dot on her forehead glitters between two large hoop earrings that fold her ears forward.

To the left of the pool is BarKockalotte's fenced training ground. He showcases his sling shot marksmanship for his lone-bear cub audience, Joecub, who struggles to cling to the fence of the training ground.

Not far from the one-dog show stands LeDrun, practicing Tai Chi under the maple tree.

A squirrel diligently digs some nuts out for afternoon snack time next to the tortoise, but accidentally hits LeDrun's bulbous noggin with an acorn.

"O-u-c-h!" LeDrun utters a slow moan.

The suspect squirrel quickly grabs his nuts and scurries up into the tree, hiding behind the enormous palm leaves and peeking out.

"Are you OK, Sweet Shell?" meows Purrplexy from the poolside. She strides toward the tortoise, like a model on a catwalk.

"I am fine. It was a hit-and-run accident. And don't sweeten me up. Sudden attitude change is a common symptom of infection by the Virus," replies LeDrun, looking up into the tree.

The squirrel is holding his breath.

"Nonsense," purrs Purrplexy, placing her soft paws gently on the tortoise's head.

"Let me see. You have a small bump on your head. But guess what? I am a certified feline massage therapist. Let me take care of you," volunteers Purrplexy, beginning to knead and press the tortoise's head with her soft paws.

"So, the crazy trips you take us on through your chest button, they are not real, right?" purrs Purrplexy, batting her fake eyelashes at LeDrun.

"But how come my fur is still charred? And look at me!" Purrplexy unveils her face. "I look like a Siamese cat! I hate Siamese, those third world uggos."

"So you care more about your look than the Virus?" mocks LeDrun as he enjoys the head massage with eyes closed.

"If you," whispers Purrplexy into LeDrun's ear, "could restore my beauty right now, I would give you a Euphoric Massage, if you know what I mean."

The certified feline masseuse touches and gropes the tortoise in a quite unprofessional way.

"Don't get all pawsy on me," reproves LeDrun.

"You see, everyone in the family has their own weak links susceptible to the Virus. It takes different approaches..." LeDrun starts nurturing the cat.

"Ah--fiddledeedee," Purrplexy interrupts LeDrun.

"Speaking of the family, it would break my heart if I spread the Virus to them. So, why don't you take me alone to the Sanctuary? Just you and me. Happily ever after. Of course, you will have to give me back my snow-white fluffy fur first. What do you think?" Purrplexy lures and tempts the death messenger.

"Hahaha! The Virus is contagious, but not through physical contact or breathing. You are one coaxing cat," LeDrun cracks up.

Barkockalotte catches the seemingly cozy scene of LeDrun and Purrplexy under the maple tree. The dog darts over and barks at the cat:

"Get your Virus-infected paws off LeDrun! What did you say to make him laugh? I am the funny pet in the family! Do you even know any theories of humor? I know all!"

"I gnaw!" squeals Joecub as he waddles over to join the gang.

"I laughed because Purrplexy has got the whole Sanctuary endeavor wrong. It is not an engineered project on how to get over THERE, but an enriching journey of returning in HERE," LeDrun points to his heart.

"What, if anything, do your breasts have to do with being rich? Duh!" mocks the cat.

"A rich life has everything to do with how we experience it. **It is an ever-growing, artistic way against an engineered, promoted method.** And could you please limit your paw contact to my head? I am not eloping with you. And your fur will grow back through its natural course," says LeDrun to Purrplexy, who is tempting him with the possibility of a happy ending.

"I have no idea what you are talking about," Purrplexy denies all charges.

She stands up, tidies up her long silk robe, puts the veil back on, and heads back toward the poolside.

BarKockalotte, however, is not done yet. He swiftly snaps the chiffon veil from the cat's face, and mocks: "Siamese! Siamese! Her face looks like burnt cheese! Brahahahah!"

The provocative dog holds the merlot-colored veil in front of Purrplexy's face, and swings it left and right like a bullfighter's red cape.

"You are a dead dog!" yowls Purrplexy. She snatches the veil, throws it on the grass, and starts chasing BarKockalotte around the backyard.

Joecub crawls under the soft, translucent piece of cloth and looks at the world through a pantyhose-filtered camera lens.

"Red!" coos the mesmerized cub, rolling around playfully.

"Boobie!" giggles Jo, pointing his tiny finger at Pilferine's roof.

"It's a wide-angle motion-censored security camera," mumbles the tortoise, and yet sounds loud and clear to BarKockalotte's ears.

"A what? Where?!" the guard dog halts his chasing and running.

In the direction of Joecub's finger, BarKockalotte catches a glimpse of a dark-brown-colored, dome-shaped glass thingy on their raccoon neighbor's rooftop.

"It blatantly violates our privacy!" barks Barkockalotte.

"Let me grab my weapon. I'll take care of it! Nobody can take advantage of our family!" He swiftly grabs his slingshot from the dog run, and gallops into the sunroom.

"Bang-bang!" Barkockalotte uses the sunroom as his bunker, hides behind the door left ajar, and fires through the crevice. The shattered glass of the dome camera on the neighboring roof announces the dog's "mission accomplished."

BarKockalotte struts out of the sunroom, wearing the slingshot on his head upside down as a green beret. On his face, a bright, triumphant grin radiates contently with pride.

**"Love guides you to discover the self; Fear guards you along the journey,"** chants LeDrun from beneath the maple tree.

He then raises his voice: "I could be wrong. Maybe it's not a security camera...could just be a regular night light or something."

"What? But who would ever put a light there?" the dog's face dims down, and his smile freezes.

"I thought you were the authority of..." BarKockalotte whimpers and mutters.

"Someone is in trouble," meows Purrplexy as she picks her veil up off the grass and puts it back on to cover her charred face. She then catwalks past BarKockalotte and raps: "Dumb ass! Dumb ass! Get whipped twice its size!"

"Mee-oww-bluuu-blaaaa-tsss ---!" Purrplexy sarcastically plays air drums along with her belittlement.

***********

A couple of days later, Polisco comes home and summons the family to the sunroom.

"Guys, I have exciting news. We got sued," announces Polisco from the black swivel chair, holding Joecub on his knees.

"Again? By whom this time? And for what?" growls PanRoo in the other chair, stroking Purrplexy in her arms.

"Pilferine. She sued us for damaging her property. If she wins, we have to pay for repairs AND the emotional agony caused by her loss. Although it is hard to imagine how deeply her emotion is attached to 'whatever' light was on her rooftop. Anyway, we would go broke if we had to pay the proposed compensation," mocks Polisco, rolling his eyes.

"So much for getting rich for the Sanctuary," PanRoo sighs, shaking her round head.

"Bang-bang-splang!" jibbers Joecub. He lowers his head, trying to find the guilty dog.

BarKockalotte pretends to sleep on the floor. He buries his head in his tail with eyes closed and ears flattened.

"Oh, stop playing dead," meows Purrplexy at BarKockalotte on the floor. "Burying your head in your butt won't get you out of trouble."

"LeDrun, help!" whimpers the dog at the meditating tortoise on the large bay windowsill.

# 17

## The F Word

"I was contemplating on the 'F' word just now. Any insights?" asks LeDrun, stretching his limbs.

"What F word? That F word?" PanRoo raises her brows.

"Oh, is that what's on your mind when you meditate and pose like a wise know-it-all?" Polisco gangs up against the magic tortoise.

"No," says LeDrun. "It is the 'F' word in Planet **F**. What do you think the 'F' stands for in Planet **F**?" inquires the death messenger from the windowsill. He lies on his side, using one arm to support his head.

"Who cares?" woofs BarKockalotte. "Let's take care of the lawsuit now!"

"Patient, doggy," smiles LeDrun, giving BarKockalotte a forehead flick through the air.

"Ou—whuua-whuaw-ou," howls the dog in pain, resting his pouty face on the floor.

"I'll start because it's a no-brainer," meows Purrplexy. "'F' stands for Feline, Planet Feline. You know who the Queen is? Purrplexy Your Majesty!" acclaims Purrplexy, stretching her body for a yawn.

"Don't flatter yourself!" woofs BarKockalotte, raising his head off the floor. "According to historians, millions of years ago, this planet was called Earth. The Earth accommodated a group of animals called Homo sapiens. However, a much more violent but less intelligent Homo species called Homo fatuus came to power. They used the advanced weapons that the Homo sapiens designed to wipe out the entire sapien species. And those Homo fatuus renamed the place Planet **F**, i.e., Planet Fatuus."

"Fat--tush," coos Joecub, dancing on his tiny tushy on his dad's knees.

"Anywho," BarKockalotte continues his lecture, "the Homo fatuus was so self-destructive that it didn't take long for them to annihilate each other to species extinction. Then a group of polar bears called the Fluffs entered the spotlight of social evolution. So, Planet **F** for fatuus became Planet **F** for Fluffs. In fact, master Pol is the royal descendent of those polar bears. Look how white and fluffy he is!" the dog simpers and wags at the polar bear.

"Exactly! Change is the middle name of social evolution," remarks PanRoo. "Aren't you all fed up with the Fluffs' ridiculous social superiority, especially the males? I think Planet **F** should stand for Planet Female because the Future is Female!" The panda kangaroo air-salutes.

"I find it comical that those words come from a woman with P-E-N-I-S envy," Polisco laughs while spelling out the word for Joecub's sake. "But I'll tell you what, I don't give a damn about social superiority. We are the bull's eye targeted by all the animal groups nowadays. Our society suffers gravely from the moral and intellectual degradation of our forefathers' heritage. Look how resentful and foolish the animals are nowadays! And don't get me started on the Virus. It's not a natural disaster. It is indeed an artificially made disease! Planet **F** has become Planet Failed or, to put it elegantly, Planet F-U-C-K-E-D," Polisco vents as usual.

"Well, speaking of animal groups," Mr. Bar chimes in, "according to the latest social science studies, we have just reached six-digits in terms of the number of different types of social groups. And the 'F' groups continue proliferating: the Flacks, the Frowns, the Fasians, the Fomos, the neoFluffs, so on and so forth." BarKockalotte analyses and euphemizes.

***"Group priority incurs outsider enemies; deferential interdependence nurturers co-growth,"*** LeDrun chants some mystic lyrics. He slowly turns to Joecub and asks: "What do YOU think the 'F' stands for, Jo?"

The cub rolls around on his dad's furry thighs, paws holding feet. He looks up in the air with slightly frowned eyebrows and a somewhat wrinkled nose. Then his body turns stiff as he holds his breath and pushes: "Blo-loo-lo-ei-er-fu--tt." A coy, versatile, wet cub fart answers the profound "F" question.

The family bursts into laughs and joyful complaints, especially from Polisco, the immediate cub fart victim.

"Nice answer, buddy! A juicy one with a pungent attitude," The proud dad praises his son.

***********

"Fart aside," LeDrun chuckles and continues, "think more deeply with your hearts about what Planet **F** means to you."

"Fame! No question!" meows Purrplexy. "I wholeheartedly believe in Fame. In this society, if you make your fame, good or bad, as long as you keep getting attention, the money will crawl its way to you like a

B-I-T-C-H. So definitely, Fame."

"Hey! Leave our female canine population alone!" barks BarKockalotte the protector.

"I would say Fortune," opines PanRoo. "On Moon Sticks, we call Planet **F** the Fortune Land. It embodies freedom, equality, and happiness. We are told that on Planet **F**, everyone has equal opportunity to make their fortune. I was surely lured by this fantasy and decided to come here to seek mine. What they didn't tell you was that the rich have already married the powerful, leaving the majority of the poor animals fighting for the leftover crumbs. Oh, how spitefully we fight! Especially against the newcomers! But in my dreams, Planet **F** is still my land of Fortune." PanRoo looks afar as if she saw the mirage of her castle up in the air.

"According to the Global Statistics Bureau…" woofs BarKockalotte.

"Listen to your own heart, not via the official loudspeakers." LeDrun reminds the dog.

"Family! Planet **F** definitely means Planet Family to me!" woofs the dog. "Family is the basic unit of society. If a family is a healing and nurturing haven for its members, so will be our society. Umm… yeah! LeDrun is family, so he will help me…us out of this lawsuit, right?" BarKockalotte raises his head, stretches his neck, opens his mouth, and starts howling.

"Quit howling, Bark-A-Lot!" grunts Polisco. "If I could ask this question to our forefathers, I bet they would tell me Planet **F** means Fight, Fortitude, and Feat. I've always admired their courage to fight for their own destiny, their strength to endure all adversities, and their unparalleled achievement of founding this great civilization. And look at us now! Weak, bitter, and selfish! We rely on AI to do most of the work, on pills to regulate our bodies, and the worst of the worst, on the government to take care of us! Where is our avant-garde legacy? Where is our entrepreneurial spirit? Shame! Shame! Shame!" Polisco lapses into his nostalgic funk again.

"F you?" asks Joecub, blinking his confused eyes towards the magic tortoise.

"Aha," laughs LeDrun lovingly. "I am frankly disturbed by your answers. The F word... the F word..." The tortoise takes out his crystal flask from his shell and savors a small sip.

***********

"Fear," articulates LeDrun, "is the F word I was contemplating earlier."

"Fear?" woofs BarKockalotte. "Why do you want to think about THAT? You are supposed to live without fear."

"Or bury it in your sandbox," Purrplexy the cat enlightens.

"I have to admit," says PanRoo, "I have plenty of fear in me. Every time I go out alone, I am afraid of being victimized by a mass shooting, road rage, hate crime, woman trafficking, robbery, rape..." the panda kangaroo lists off the frequent crimes in town.

"Because you are a pansy," disapproves Polisco. "I am fearless! Nobody and nothing can scare me on this planet, not even the Virus. It's all fake news!"

"Ewws!" cheerleads Jo the cub on his daddy's belly.

"I don't know," frowns PanRoo. "Pilferine's husband did kill himself. And when the doctor showed me the bullet that they dug out of your chest last year, it looked pretty real to me."

"You've all misunderstood Fear," elucidates LeDrun. "***Fear is self-preservation, the immediate Guard of your Essence, a natural*** *escort on your life journey."*

"Without Fear, you wouldn't survive, nor would you have clarity about the world around you. Do you still remember the Origin and the life messenger PaGoo?" LeDrun smiles at the thought of his former work buddy.

"You mean the ball of goo and the giant who juggles crystal flasks with her boobs bouncing?" Polisco has a photographic memory, selectively.

"Watch your mouth," LeDrun gives the polar bear a stern look. "The two flasks in the life messenger's hands contain Love and Fear. She charges Love and Fear into every soon-to-be-born baby in order to prepare them for the new life journey ahead and the new world around them. **On the journey of self-discovery, Love sheds light on your Essence like a phare while Fear patrols your surroundings like an escort. Love guides. Fear guards.**"

LeDrun floats back onto the windowsill and returns to meditating.

All of a sudden, BarKockalotte recalls something important. He trots towards the floating tortoise, sits down, hangs his tongue out, smiles, and breathes in LeDrun's face.

"Ugh...kuh...kun," coughs LeDrun while withholding his breath. "Oral hygiene, doggy."

"I was wondering." BarKockalotte wags his tail. "Now that we answered your question about the 'F' word, could you take care of the lawsuit now?"

"My place," says LeDrun with one eye open. "In fact, it's my work lair. Each death messenger has a special place to take care of business. That place settles all cases." The tortoise breaks out the crystal flask and starts guzzling.

"Your lair?" shouts Purrplexy. "I knew you were a devil!" The scared cat hides her head in PanRoo's chest.

"Wrong," corrects LeDrun. "A devil lives off your Energy, like the Virus. A death messenger returns your Essence to the Origin, to be reborn."

"What are we waiting for then? Let's check out your lair, and more importantly, take care of the case!" hurrays BarKockalotte, nodding like a bobble head on the dashboard of a car that has driven over an unexpected speed hump.

"Paws on my chest. I need to get my claws wet again. It's been a while since that night at Pilferine's," recollects LeDrun, putting the empty flask back in his shell.

"I'm ok. You guys can go," meows Purrplexy, licking her fur. "I need to heal my burns…"

"Mr. Bar?" Polisco snaps his fingers, a mafia gesture code between the master and the dog.

"Yes, sir!" salutes BarKockalotte merrily.

He swiftly blindfolds Purrplexy and puts a ball of dirty sock in her mouth. The dog then grabs the cat's paw and presses it on top of the tortoise's chest.

"Feline abduction! Someone call the police!" yowls and squirms the cat victim.

"The Police are right here," sneers Polisco.

"Does your work lair have a name like the **I** Resort?" asks PanRoo among the hullabaloo.

"My big **D** Lair," replies LeDrun with a subtle trace of pride.

# 18

## The D Lair

The animals find themselves inside a magnificent glass dome structure built over water. At the center of the building erects a glowy purple pedestal, upon which LeDrun meditates. A circle of round, opaque glass doors encompass the pedestal like a bodyguards' eagle eyes.

Through the glass ceiling, the group can see storm clouds building up. Clouds render waves of color as they fight each other for position, from slate gray to ink black. Purple lightning crawls up from the horizon like slithering serpents, rapidly infesting the entire sky, and drooping back down, one after another onto the meridians of the hemispherical glass building.

All of a sudden, a bolt of blinding lightning strikes the zenith of the dome and instantaneously transmits a cylindrical beam of energy to the top of the pedestal, where LeDrun glows like an orange ember. Meanwhile, a resounding crack of thunder shakes the building, reverberating like a massive explosion.

"I bet the tortoise is toasted," figures Polisco, arms crossed.

"If I bark loud enough, it will counteract the thunder!" BarKockalotte applies his theory by barking his dog heart out.

"Shuu-op! Shuut up! Shut the F--kup!" yowls Purrplexy at the dog while spitting the dirty sock ball out of her mouth and un-blindfolding herself.

Between nature's wrath and the animals' clamor, LeDrun floats up, beaming into the air: "Ladies and gentlemen, welcome to my big **D** Lair!"

"Come on! Call it the **D** Lair, just like the **I** Resort. Stop saying 'your big' **D** Lair. It's overcompensating, you loser," mumbles Polisco, clearly offended.

"Boo!" yowls Purrplexy. "I hate scary haunted houses! You'd better not make us walk through this place!"

"It's my work lair," introduces LeDrun. "'**D**' stands for Death, not that other thing, Pol. Look at those doors around me. They are Death Portals."

The death messenger levitates around a perimeter of opaque glass doors that encircle the pedestal.

"What Death Portals? Didn't you just get struck by lightening? How come you are not barbecued like Lexy? With that powerful electrical voltage, at least some part of you has to shrivel like your turkey neck. Flaccid...accid...cid...dd..." Polisco pokes fun at the tortoise by jiggling his wrinkly neck skin.

As if LeDrun's neck was charged by the lightning, the mouthy polar bear gets electrocuted. All of his white fur erects like a porcupine. Eyes wide open and body frozen, smoke billows from his head.

"You see the purple lightning encircling the lair?" LeDrun points skyward while suppressing a laugh. "Those are death signals carried by Fear-charged Energy. But not all death signals indicate actual deaths. Most of them are simply rendered upon the thoughts of death.

The lightning that just struck the signal receptor on my chest, in fact, signaled an actual death," explains the death messenger.

"What happens after you receive an actual death signal?" inquires PanRoo out of curiosity.

"Upon the reception of such a death signal, a death messenger will immediately trace it back to the sender by following the Fear signal's origin in the universe. Depending on the cause of the death, natural or unnatural, disease or murder, one of the Death Portals will open up a cosmic temporospatial passage and take the death messenger to either a biosphere or sociosphere wherein the death occurred. I bet right now one of my colleagues is at the death site already. Ah, I hate to admit it, but I miss work sometimes," reminisces LeDrun.

"So, why did you bring us here? To watch how you work? I thought you were still healing and recuperating. Isn't it too soon for you to get back to work?" asks PanRoo, feeling the impending empty pouch syndrome already.

"I am not going back to work anytime soon," assures LeDrun. "After the incident at Pilpherine's and the impossible revival from it, I now have a loftier mission. I want to save you and hopefully everyone else from the Virus. And in order to beat the Virus, understanding Love and Fear and how they charge and direct your Energy is a fundamental step."

"So both Love and Fear can charge Energy?" woofs BarKockalotte.

"Yes," confirms the death messenger. "Before you were born, PaGoo endowed you with both Love charge and Fear charge in a primordial equilibrium. Once you enter the world of endless stimulation, your Love or Fear would intuitively charge your Energy to act and react in the form of thoughts, feelings, words, actions, and more.

Sending out a death signal is the grand finale of one's Fear charge before it exhausts all options to protect you. Death messengers are Fear experts. Thank you very much. No need for applause. We can detect Fear Energy of all sorts and all magnitudes emitted from anybody," LeDrun proudly proclaims.

"So you know nothing about Love." PanRoo quickly points out.

"I have my secret supply chain in the Origin." The magic tortoise winks as he breaks out the crystal flask.

"You mean you whore yourself out to PaGoo in exchange for… meow-ouch!" Purrplexy is somehow electrocuted as well before she finishes her sentence.

The death messenger levitates around and about the family, stretches out his neck and sniffs off the crowns of the family's fluffy heads to search for signs of Fear.

"Buzz off!" Polisco waves his bear paw above his head as if LeDrun were a buzzing insect hovering about. "I don't have any fear. Quit sniffing! I am not afraid of anything!"

He stands tall with arms akimbo as if he were ready to save the world.

"That's a lie," remarks LeDrun.

The death messenger then floats in front of the polar bear, stretching his long neck toward Polisco's face as if he were about to give him a diplomatic kiss. He smiles graciously: "I dare you to touch my neck again."

"Ummm… no, thanks. I am go…good," stutters Polisco, taking a step backward.

"See? That's how Fear protects you. Always be true to yourself. Don't live in preferred illusions," enlightens LeDrun,

"I think my biggest fear is getting killed in a hate crime in that hostile town of ours," frowns PanRoo.

"My biggest fear is failing to protect my masters," groans BarKockalotte, recollecting his late master's traumatic death. He takes out the sling shot and rubs it.

"Bang! Bang! Splang!" seeing the slingshot, Joecub gets excited.

"My biggest fear is that I cannot make it and die an ordinary cat. Life is short, especially for a cat. Grrr, I wish I was a tortoise," meows and pouts Purrplexy.

Then all the animals turn their heads toward Polisco. The cornered polar bear engages in eye contact with LeDrun.

"An honest answer?" asks Polisco.

"Always," encourages LeDrun.

"Fine," Polisco raises his voice. "My biggest fear is to lose my E-R-E-C-T-I-O-N, period."

Polisco's answer incites another animal hullaballoo, among which Mr. Bar raises the loudest and bitterest protest.

"Love and Fear, the intrinsic Guide and Guard on the self-discovery journey," murmurs LeDrun from the column pedestal, "**Love inspires you to connect with the world for essential realization; Fear enlightens you to break away from situations for vital preservation.**"

# 19

## Fear Bubble

The death messenger floats in a circle around the family, raises his claws, and snaps his fingers as if he were performing an exotic dance. Mysteriously, five transparent, delicate, flowy bouncing bubbles of different sizes line up in front of the animals.

"Bubbles!" Joecub's face lights up, as the cub loves blowing bubbles in the park.

"What are those bubbles for? Are we going to play a bubble shooting game?" woofs BarKockalotte, taking out his slingshot and aiming at the bubbles.

"They are called 'Fear bubbles,'" LeDrun gives the dog a side eye. "Like Love balloons, Fear bubbles will take you on an excursion through those Death Portals."

The death messenger points around the encircling corridor of round, opaque glass doors that surround the glowy purple pedestal.

"Death Portals that lead to death scenes? No! Thank you!" yowls Purrplexy, back arching, fur erecting.

"Don't worry, kitten. The Fear bubble will protect you," comforts LeDrun. "Whenever you perceive risks, danger or threats out there, the Fear bubble will create a 'safe zone' for you. Are you ready?"

"A safe zone? How?" questions Polisco. "These bubbles look no firmer than those large soapy ones in the park."

Polisco sticks his stubby finger out in attempt to probe the porous, membrane-like surface of a Fear bubble, but retracts his paw upon second thought.

"It's another trap," chatters Purrplexy. "So, I am like traveling through this creepy haunted lair inside this bubble? Are you sure the bubble is going to protect me? Because the last time I trusted you with the Love balloon, look what happened to me!" pouts Purrplexy, pointing at her charred facial fur.

"In fact, YOU are to protect yourself," rectifies LeDrun. "Fear is your intrinsic Guard that you are endowed with from the Origin. It empowers you to survive in the world that you were delivered into. When necessary, Fear charges your Energy and fashions it into various weapons. *Fear is to surviving as Love is to thriving.*"

"I don't know," Polisco shakes his fluffy bear head. "Fear still sounds like something for pansies." He glances at PanRoo. "I am not easily scared or panicked. I am pretty strong."

"Nah," LeDrun shakes his bulbous head. "Fear is not weakness. It's in fact the source of your strength."

> *Fear is vigilance*
> *Observation and knowledge*
> *Mindfulness and agility*
> *The essential understanding of the world*
> *As well as the environing of others*

When Fear discerns risk or detects danger, it charges up your Energy for self-defense. And as for scare and panic, it is due to your ignorance of your inner Guard and the estrangement from your own

Fear Energy."

The animals are puzzled and discombobulated.

***********

"So, what are the 'Fear bubbles' for again?" PanRoo draws air quotation marks.

"It blows!" squeals Joecub, whose mind is fixated on blowing bubbles.

"Fear bubbles," reveals LeDrun, "like Love balloons, will help you perceive your Fear from the INSIDE. You see the soft, membrane-like surface of the bubble? It is a metaphorical projector that exhibits how your Fear charges Energy and fashions it into self-protection weapons: distancing, armoring, camouflaging, shielding, blocking, attacking, etcetera, whenever you sense risk or face danger along the road."

"Well, at least we are going together, right?" moans and groans BarKockalotte, tail between legs.

"No." LeDrun shakes his head. He floats back onto the glowy purple column pedestal and points at the circle of doors around the family.

"You see the Death Portals around you? Each one of you will take a unique passage to be sent on your own adventure. The D Lair is a spherical building, a semi-biosphere and a semi-sociosphere. That is to say, you may end up in the vast wilderness or in a densely populated town. We don't know which one yet, but the Fear bubble is about to take you there through one of those Portals. Remember: there is a fat chance you will run into each other in the sphere. Now, close your eyes and ponder on the unknown world that awaits behind those doors. Do you feel that all your senses are in high gear already?"

LeDrun the death messenger attempts to incite fear among the family.

"I am not leaving without my cub!" roars PanRoo, holding Joecub tightly in her arms.

"I'll take care of him," assures LeDrun.

"Parents are the world of your young cubs. If you don't understand your own Magic Powers, you become susceptible to the Virus. If you were infected with the Virus, you would tragically create an inhospitable environment for the cubs. Consequently, your poor cubs have to spend so much Fear Energy to protect themselves from you, and yet have very limited Love Energy to thrive," enlightens the magic tortoise.

He reaches his right claw into the air and grabs a sparkling bubble blower toy. He then uses his left claw to gently tap on the surface of the pedestal top where Joecub suddenly appears, beaming and clapping.

"But…" hesitates PanRoo. As she attempts to reach for the pedestal, a Fear bubble floats toward the panda kangaroo. It gently but swiftly envelops her and carries her away through one of the open opaque glass doors, closing swiftly behind her.

"Master Pan! No way! I am not going by myself! Master Pol!" barks and whimpers BarKockalotte. As he implores Polisco to let him tag along in the **D** Lair excursion, a Fear bubble quickly envelops him and whisks him away down to a different path.

"Motherfrukers! Stop looting my family!" roars Polisco. Before more profanity can utter from his foul mouth, the polar bear is wrapped up inside a Fear bubble and vanishes behind a Death Portal door.

Meanwhile, Purplexy climbs onto the pedestal and tightly hugs

LeDrun from behind. "I am not going inside the haunted house! I bet there is a slaughter room somewhere with a serial cat killer waiting to cut me up with an electric chainsaw!" yowls the cat.

Her sharp claws are lodged firmly under the edge of the tortoiseshell while a Fear bubble is trying to take her.

Feeling the pain, LeDrun turns around and blows a breath onto Purrplexy's face.

Seemingly tranquilized, the cat gives up and launches her adventure through another door.

"Ouch, my back hurts," LeDrun utters a slow moan. He then breaks out his flask from inside his tortoiseshell and guzzles up.

"Let's blow some bubbles in the town park." The tortoise smiles at Joecub as they sit on the pedestal.

Upon LeDrun's words, one of the round opaque glass doors opens ajar. The death messenger, carrying the cub on his shell, vanishes from the lair.

# 20

## Desert Oasis

Polisco opens his eyes in a desert. A dust storm has just passed. The sun seems wounded, oozing out bloody lava-like waves that slowly colonize the slate-colored clouds in the sky. The thick lava paint then drips down from the sky, and clings to the winding crests of endless sand dunes. The world is dead silent and yet carnival loud.

Through the Fear bubble's transparent membrane, Polisco feels the scorching heat of the sand transmitting from his large bear feet up to his stubby legs.

"This is excruciating, a polar bear in a hot desert! I think that tortoise is a sadist," grumbles Polisco.

As if the death messenger heard his complaint, a gust of cold wind whistles a gruesome song, blowing into his ears, trickling down through his veins, and pounding urgently on his bladder.

Nevertheless, Polisco notices something strange inside him.

"If there were a magic pill that could optimize all my abilities, this is how it would feel," observes Pol.

He notices that the world has somehow become brighter and clearer. He can see things deemed trivial, hear things considered negligible, and smell things held insignificant.

"Fear is not all bad after all," contemplates Pol. "I've never been so vigilant and attentive, which I need the most to survive in this grisly desert."

A faint rustling sound from the sand catches Polisco's attention. He scans the perimeter but does not see a thing.

"Maybe just wind," says Pol to himself.

But the sound continues and gets nearer. All of a sudden, he hears a hiss. Following the hiss, he sees a horned desert viper flicking her fork-shaped tongue in and out, sidewinding toward him.

"Sf...k!" swears Pol. "Her venom could kill 10 polar bears! Should I run? No. I heard that most snakes need reading glasses to see well. So, if I stayed still and looked tough, she would probably take me for a rock."

Upon his thought, Polisco notices that his Fear bubble begins hardening up. The bubble's soft, breathable membrane turns into a tough, steely, tempered-glass-like polar bear armor.

"Yes! Bra...hahah" Polisco laughs out loud. "Bite me now, you long skinny turd!"

The wave of Polisco's laughter reverberates through the air and is caught by the viper's radar. She suddenly raises her horned head from the sand, together with one third of her body. A Fear buddle blows up from nowhere, enveloping the desert viper like an inflatable snow globe.

"It looks like her Fear bubble is triggered too." Polisco is intrigued.

Looking through his Fear bubble and into hers, the polar bear detects vigilance in the snake's eyes.

"Ok. I am not moving. You just wiggle on." Pol aims to communicate this message to the snake via eye contact.

But the horned desert viper stands still. She tilts her head slightly and quickly glances at a sand burrow next to Polisco's right foot.

Polisco follows the snake's vision trajectory and lays his eyes on a circle of eggs thinly covered in sand.

"Ops! Sorry!" Polisco recognizes his intrusion. "I'd better back off."

Heeding the polar bear's energy, the Fear bubble resumes its softness and drags Polisco away from mother viper's babies.

"I am pretty sure that she is waving her horns at me to say thank you," smiles Polisco, waving at the desert viper as he retreats backward.

"Everyone has a Fear bubble," ponders Polisco. "You just have to pay attention."

The polar bear treks through the desert and greets various Fear bubbles, inside which reside lizards, scorpions, spiders, insects and more.

"I need some water before I turn into dried fruit." Polisco licks his chapped lips.

Upon this thought, a desert oasis crops up among the dunes.

***********

The oasis is like an oval green gem embedded in the lava-tinted desert. Surrounded by some tall palm trees and thick bushes, two deep dark ponds stare at the sky like two inferno eyes. Animals that inhabit the oasis form an intricate symbiosis, and also pose potential danger to any newcomers.

Polisco is thrilled at the sight of the oasis. He somersaults down the dune and rolls up to the pond bank. He again feels Fear, the strange vigilance inside.

"Wait." Polisco withholds his impulse to jump into the pond. "I'd better check. A crocodile may be lurking in the water. I hate big mouth animals, those overambitious predators."

Pol takes one step back on the bank and starts checking around. Distant but clear, he hears a laugh, a desert hyena laugh. Tracing the sound wave of the laughter, behind some thorny bushes, Polisco sees a clan of spotted hyenas. Their large signature ears are like double belled bulb horns, blaring about their territorial sovereignty.

"Oh! I hate those nasty animals," grumbles Pol. "They attack your anus."

Polisco's rear end clinches.

"Because they tend to gang up and prey on the weak, I'd better stand tall and buff to show them who the boss is!"

At such a thought, Polisco observes that his Fear bubble expands, which projects a bigger and fluffier image of the polar bear to the hyenas.

The clan of hyenas clearly catches the sight of the large white furry intruder. All of a sudden, a collective Fear bubble inflates and sucks in all the clan members. As they blast vocal warning messages at Polisco, one hyena breaks through the collective Fear bubble and dashes towards the polar bear.

"Holy shit! I am gonna be attacked!" figures Polisco.

Heeding the Fear Energy, Pol's Fear bubble again turns into a hard, steely, and tempered-glass-like armor with double shields on his butt.

"It's me! Your Pancakes!" whoop-whoops the hyena in a hushed PanRoo voice as she approaches Polisco.

Inside his armor, Polisco looks into the hyena's eyes. They are full of joy and affection. But when he moves his eyeballs around, Pol sees an animal with two trumpet-like ears and spotted fur. The armored polar bear is confused: "Pansy? What happened to you?"

"Shush! It's my camouflage," reveals PanRoo.

"I went through the Death Portal and woke up in the oasis. A clan of hyenas immediately found me and started laughing at me. I freaked out inside my Fear bubble and thought to myself: 'They laugh at me because I look different. I wish I looked more like them.' And somehow, the Fear bubble projected my image as a hyena. How's my make-believe façade? Pretty real, right?" PanRoo shakes her trumpet ears to show off.

"Oh, come on! You are half bear for heaven's sake!" shouts Polisco in disdain.

"They laugh at you? Punch them. Kick them. Roar at them! Why in the hell would you choose to imitate them? Nobody respects imitators! Not to mention that they are merciless predators, and you are a vegetarian. How long can you stay in disguise, huh? Are you going to hunt with them and eat other animals' flesh and guts? Look at you! Ugly as hell!" roars the frustrated polar bear.

"Hey!" PanRoo is offended. "LeDrun said Fear charges Energy to protect us with different weapons. Yours might be a tough armor. I choose camouflage. It doesn't mean that I'm weak. You don't get to judge how I protect myself!"

As the couple quarrels, the clan of hyenas marches toward them like a spotted army, blaring their loudest laughter.

"Camouflage my ass," Polisco purses his lips and rolls his eyes. "What are they saying?"

"Darn it! They're all yelling 'Catch the traitor'!" interprets PanRoo.

"Screw it. I am not one of you!" growls PanRoo at the laughing hyenas. Heeding her energy, PanRoo's Fear bubble resumes its transparent membrane, as PanRoo reappears in her natural form of a panda kangaroo.

"I am dangerously dehydrated. I don't think I can last," gags the polar bear.

PanRoo pauses for a second. "Swim across the pond. A polar bear and a panda kangaroo can outswim the hyenas. And drink some pond water while you are in there."

After quickly exchanging eye contact, the bears jump into the pond.

Maybe PanRoo has overestimated her swimming skills, or Polisco's armor is as heavy as rocks. Like a determined suicidal couple, they plummet straight downward under the water, only to realize that the pond seems bottomless.

# 21

## Sighted Blindness

Pan and Pol regain their bearings in a splash pad at a park. Baby animals are screaming and laughing and chasing each other in the water. Their parents stand by, complaining about the subpar park facilities and hot weather.

"How did we get here?" asks PanRoo with a puzzled look.

"That darn pond is like a bottomless water slide. My bottom hurts," PanRoo struggles to stand up under a mushroom spray fountain.

"The pond has to be the inside passage or something that connects the biosphere and the sociosphere in the **D** Lair," reckons Polisco, shaking water off his matted fur.

"We must be in the sociosphere now. Look at this park. It's as noisy and shitty as our town park. Good! Because I hate nature! Nighnight desert and hyenas! Ou! My head!" The polar bear stands up and gives PanRoo a high five, but bumps his head against the mushroom head.

The bear couple leaves the splash pad and stroll arm in arm through the park. Their Fear bubbles adjoin each other like a squeezed infinity symbol.

Somehow, they feel safe.

"I need to find a urinal," says Polisco, searching around.

"One second dehydrated, urgent to pee the next." PanRoo smiles and yet shakes her head.

"I drank a lot of water in the damn pond!" Pol defends himself.

As they search for a public bathroom for the polar bear, a small amphitheater catches their attention. Some audience members throw trash and water bottles onto the stage while others boo and hiss. And at the center of the stage stands an espresso-colored glass box, inside of which Purrplexy is performing tasteless erotic dance.

"That's indeed inappropriate!" roars PanRoo.

The bear couple hops onto the stage.

"Stop it, Lexy! You are embarrassing yourself!" yells and points PanRoo with her index finger. It is master Pan's signal for the pets at home to stop fooling around.

The cat, however, can perceive neither the masters nor the audience outside her box.

Polisco squats down, examining the dark colored glass box.

"It seems that Lexy's glass box is made of two-way glass: the interior is reflective like a mirror, but the exterior is clear glass that allows us to see her performing. Why would the silly cat do that?" reckons and questions Polisco.

"I think her Fear bubble protects her with some kind of detachment," remarks Pan.

"Look how zoned out she is!" observes Pol. "Like when you put your headset on in a public place, or just mentally turn off the world around you. You're a teacher. You must be familiar with those students who are physically present but mentally absent." Pol makes a face at Pan.

"Or a self-indulgent, emotionally unavailable spouse," PanRoo retaliates.

Polisco ignores PanRoo's complaint. He jumps onto the stage and picks up the two-way glass cat box.

Weathering the loud protests of the audience, the bear couple flees the scene.

\*\*\*\*\*\*\*\*\*\*\*

The bear couple stops at a public bathroom. Leaving the glass cat box with Pan outside, Polisco opens the bathroom door with a loud cracking sound.

The inside is dim. Pol's nostrils and eyes are immediately assaulted by a hodgepodge of pungent smells and air-borne chemicals.

"All the park bathrooms smell alike, even the one in a lair," grumbles the bear.

The polar bear holds his breath and concentrates in front of a rusty urinal.

"A-aa—aaa!" with a whistle-like scream, PanRoo bangs the door wide open and rushes in.

Her Fear buddle envelops both the panda kangaroo and the cat.

"What the fruck!" Pol gets startled and pauses the bodily liquid discharge, leaving a very confused thingy hanging in there.

"Ri...rio...riots! A mob...shooting... in the park!...kuh! kuh! kuh!" Pan shouts with fright and coughs as she gasps and breathes in a handsome amount of the bathroom air.

"What?!" Before Polisco can ask more questions, dozens of animals squeeze through the door along with the shrilling police sirens.

Each animal appears inside the membrane of a Fear bubble.

All of a sudden, the men's room looks like the inside of a pomegranate.

Polisco observes his Fear bubble turning into a tough, steely, tempered-glass-like armor again. He elbows through the Fear bubbles of other animals and stands in front of the tiny bathroom window.

Through the spotted and blurry glass, Pol catches a mob of jackals fighting against the police who are carrying shields. The police spray tear gas and fire rubber bullets, whereas the gang throws rocks and bottles and whatnot.

Among the riots, BarKockalotte hides behind a large jackal and shoots with his slingshot.

"Ou..wuu..ou!" the dog yelps loudly as he gets hit in the eyes by the tear gas.

"It's Bark-A-Lot! He is hit!" roars Polisco, thrusting through the Fear bubbles towards the door.

PanRoo follows him, holding the glass cat box in her arms.

"Is that Siamese cat touching herself in that box?" a murmur comes from the crowd.

Pol and Pan anxiously exit the bathroom door to find themselves back in the original spot in the lair where a glowy purple pedestal is erected under the dome glass roof.

BarKockalotte leans against the pedestal, groaning with eyes closed.

LeDrun and Joecub sit next to the wounded dog.

"The dog is temporally blinded. Time to go home," says LeDrun with a grave face.

# 22

# Infected Dog

The animals return to the sunroom. BarKockalotte moans and groans on the floor. Polisco puts some eye drops in the wounded dog's eyes, only to cause louder wailing and bawling with tear bullets shooting out of his eyes. Meanwhile, Joecub cries out loud next to the dog to offer emotional support. PanRoo picks up the crying cub and takes a seat in one of the swivel chairs. Among the chaos, LeDrun meditates on the windowsill. Next to the tortoise, Purrplexy attentively washes her charred face.

"Gee, what happened to the thug dog?" meows the clueless cat.

"What happened? Ask the Bulbous Head!" roars Polisco, taking the other swivel chair.

"First a burnt cat and then a blinded dog. Are you sure you are here to save us?" PanRoo frowns and questions the meditating death messenger.

**"No push without being pushed**," articulates LeDrun, slowly opening his eyes. **"No attack without counterattack. Direct or boomerang."**

"Quit the nonsense," grunts Polisco. "You didn't take us to your creepy lair to hurt us, did you? What was the point?"

"The point," sighs LeDrun, standing up on the windowsill. "The point was to rectify Fear, the innate Guard that you were born with to protect you. And yet, in your society, Fear is mostly misunderstood by individuals and thus easily manipulated by the Virus. Without full awareness of Fear and Fear-charged Energy, you wouldn't be alerted when the Virus creeps inside you and steals your Energy for its own replication."

"Bubbles!" squeals Joecub, pouting up his lips and blowing the air. Silence.

"Well, when I go through a Death Portal and end up in a desert. I get extremely vigilant," admits Polisco, picking his round black nose.

"You know, sometimes you dream of taking a magic pill so you can just know everything. I kinda felt that way. That's how I sensed the mother viper and got the hell out of her way," says the polar bear with contentment.

**"Fear is the essential vigilance, your survival instinct,"** enlightens LeDrun.

"Fear patrols intuitively along your life journey. For every step you take, Fear checks and detects the surroundings to ensure your safety. It is diligent and constant. Endowed from the Origin, Fear is your loyal escort, dependable protector, the innate Guard on your way to self-discovery."

"I thought Fear makes us cowards," frowns PanRoo, shaking her head at the moaning dog on the floor.

"The opposite," rectifies LeDrun. "Love and Fear are called Magic Powers because they are extremely powerful. Whenever your Fear discerns risks or impending danger along the road, it charges up your Energy to take protective measures. Fear is your natural arsenal."

Standing on the windowsill, LeDrun makes a Tai Chi motion to illustrate how Fear protects: he raises his arms on both sides to form a semi-circle, halts them at eye level and pushes his palms forward with a heavy exhale.

"Tai Chi is useless," chatters Purrlexy next to the tortoise. "It can't protect anyone. It would just turn a blind eye to the surroundings. They are negligible peripherals. No care. No scare. No Fear."

The cat jumps down onto Polisco's thighs. She curls up into a ball, turns her chin up and covers one eye with her paw.

"Well, ignoring leads to ignorance. That's hardly what Fear does to guard your Essence," disagrees LeDrun. "Fear is vigilance, mindfulness, agility, strength, resistance, tolerance, respect, deference…etc. Without Fear, you would not understand the half of what's happening around you."

"Stop blithering empty words," grunts Polisco. "I'm not totally convinced that Fear can protect us. It sometimes makes me feel like peeing."

"Haha!" laughs LeDrun. "**Fear takes many forms as Love radiates in multiple colors**. That's why you need the help of a Fear bubble in my big **D** Lair. Like the Love balloon, a Fear bubble projects how Fear charges your Energy and fashions it into various weapons for self-defense. Also like a Love balloon in everyday life, a Fear bubble is a Fear-charged Energy field inside and around you, which others can perceive and recognize. Opposite the Love-charged Energy field that attracts other Love balloons, the Fear-charged Energy field is designed to repel others for safety concerns."

The death messenger then chants:

### *Colors of Love*

*Forms of Fear*
*Infinite and innate*
*Nature's intricate design*

"Is tear gas Nature's design too?" grumbles and mumbles Bar-Kockalotte on the floor.

\*\*\*\*\*\*\*\*\*\*\*

"Close your eyes and go back to your **D** Lair excursions," instructs LeDrun from the windowsill. "How did your Fear bubble change its form to protect you when you perceived danger?"

"I think mine transformed into a tough armor on me," reflects Polisco. "It made me feel bigger and stronger."

"Mine camouflaged me," PanRoo raises her paw, sitting in the other swivel chair. "My Fear bubble turned into an image of a hyena among a gang of dozens. I was less noticeable and more acceptable by appearing like them. Nobody picked on me that way. Smart hide!"

"In that amphitheater," meows Purrplexy, "when I sensed that some animals in the audience didn't like my art on stage, my Fear bubble turned into a two-way glass box. It was just what I needed: the inside of the box was a cubical of mirrors that allowed me to appreciate my own talent and beauty; and yet the outside of the box was see-through glass so that others could see my extraordinary performance. I didn't have to endure any criticism from the insignificant audience. They are nobody. I am the star." Purrplexy closes her eyes and chins up as if she were bathing in the spotlight on a stage.

"Your two-way glass box also blocked me and Pan," says Polisco, patting the cat with his booger fingers.

"There are many forms of Fear," remarks LeDrun. "On some occasions, the Fear Energy can toughen you up to show sovereignty and power. Under other circumstances, the Fear Energy executes a strategic retreat with respect. Sometimes, your Fear Energy chooses to disguise you as somebody else. Other times, it blocks harmful surroundings and breaks ties with toxic relations. And in rare cases, Fear will charge an army of your Energy to fight against an invasion. That is to say, someone or something somehow gets INSIDE your Fear bubble. That's the Guard's last resort before it sends out a death signal to the cosmos."

"What's a Fear bubble intrusion? Like a home invasion?" inquires PanRoo, patting the cub in her arms.

"Bubble pop!" coos Joecub, climbing down his mother's knees and crawling onto the floor towards BarKockalotte.

"It is similar to a sovereignty invasion by a foreign force. Remember how you triggered the collective Fear bubble of the hyenas in the oasis? You were a foreign intruder to them," LeDrun reminds the panda kangaroo. "Individuals sometimes have to face sovereignty invasions as well. For a society, you have military force for national defense; for an individual, you have Fear Energy to fight against the intrusion."

"That's what I did!" the wounded dog struggles to open his red teary eyes. "I fought hard against the cops! Look what I got!"

"No. No. No," the death messenger shakes his bulbous head. "What you did with your Fear Energy was not for self-defense because nobody was even close to your Fear bubble in that park, not to mention getting INSIDE it. What you did was aggression, the violent abuse of Fear Energy that exposed you to dangerous counterforce. Aggression only incurs self-destruction, which gets back at you, sometimes immediately, and other times with a boomerang effect. And it was definitely not your innate Guard. Something has messed up your Fear charge. It's probably the Virus."

"Ahhhhh..." the family gasps at the shocking news that the dog is infected with the Virus.

***********

"You set me up!" BarKockalotte blames the tortoise with gushing tears. "I don't have any Virus! I just didn't know anybody in that town! It was scary!"

"Oh! Don't blame the toilet for your constipation," jeers Purrplexy. "You have always been a violent, thug dog!"

"Hey! LeDrun, smoky cat called you a toilet!" reports BarKockalotte.

"The first time you used your slingshot, what did it incur?" LeDrun ignores the childish game and asks the dog a question instead.

"A lawsuit!" Polisco answers for him.

"But you said that it was a security camera! I meant to protect our family privacy!" the canine defendant justifies his act.

"So, you didn't really know what it was before taking an aggressive action. Ok. The second time you used your slingshot, what did it incur?" LeDrun continues.

"A blind dog!" Purrplexy dances like a cheerleader.

"Fighting consumes a tremendous amount of Energy," sighs LeDrun on the windowsill. "And Fear only charges your Energy for it in the case of invasion. That is, when the boundary of your Fear bubble is violated. But in your cases, you didn't give your natural Guard a chance to protect you. I believe the Virus somehow hijacked your Fear charge."

"There is no Virus!" denies BarKockalotte. "I went through the

Death Portal and ended up in a town park. I was scared, and then a party of jackals approached me. They had a good organization, and their pamphlets quoted a lot of statistics and famous animals throughout history! Most importantly, they had a lead wolf! Everybody worshiped him. And it made me feel super safe to have a leader to follow. In return, I showed him my allegiance."

"You mean you are a blind follower? Oops, pun intended," teases PanRoo, swiveling in the round chair.

A bell rings in BarKockalotte's mind among the family laughter.

His teary eyes move left and right like weaving shuttles on a loom.

He then scooches near the magic tortoise and woofs: "was it abused Fear Energy that drove Pilferine to throw your 'corpse' over her fence?"

The darkest moment of LeDrun's life flashes back.

*Surviving is co-surviving*
*Growing is co-growing.*
*Understanding dispositions*
*That's how Fear protects*

The death messenger disappears into his chants.

# 23

## Lost Cause

It is a drizzling late Saturday morning. Dark clouds transform the sky into a pressurized mister system at an outdoor party, cooling everyone down from the hot sizzling summer. Star Valley seems stoned and intoxicated, slouching sluggishly with a silly smile.

The family's sunroom has never been so quiet. BarKockalotte wears a pair of red recovery goggles, resting his head on his front paws with eyes closed. Purrplexy sits on the windowsill, frustrated with the green cone on her neck. The charred spots begin to grow new fur, making her want to scratch and lick all the time. Polisco is watching a snowball game in the living room, one paw holding a beer, the other in his crouch.

"Daddy! Play!" coos Joecub on the couch.

"Let me watch the game, Poop Child," Polisco's eyeballs are fixated on the TV screen. "Go play with Bark-A-Lot."

Joecub waddles into the sunroom.

"Mr. Bar! Play!" squeals the cub at the lying dog.

"I can't, buddy," woofs BarKockalotte from the floor.

"My eyes are still healing. I don't have good vision, nor enough energy to chase anything. Maybe the cat can entertain you? She claims that she's a professional feline entertainer, whatever that means," mocks the dog.

Joecub climbs on the windowsill.

"Lexy! Play!" pleads the cub.

"I can't, sweetie," purrs Purrplexy, looking outside through the window.

"My burns are healing. The devil's itch, you know? And with this ugly green neck cone, I cannot even walk in a straight line. Have you seen a drunk cat walk?" complains the cat.

"On second thought," Purrplexy smiles at the innocent cub. "Let's play a game called: scratch Lexy's back!"

The cat turns her back towards Joecub.

"How dare you exploit the cub!" barks BarKockalotte from down on the floor.

"Oh! Shut your bone hole!" yowls the cat at the dog. "Had LeDrun not taken care of the lawsuit, you would have been in jail by now! You know what would happen to you in there?"

Purrplexy holds her front paws to make an ever-enlarging circle in the air.

"Quiet! You two!" roars Polisco from the living room.

"Master Pol! BarKockalotte is harassing me while I am taking care of the cub!" Purrplexy tells on the dog.

"Stretch...back!" squeals Joecub, scratching the cat's back.

Polisco mumbles as he stands up and then reluctantly saunters into the sunroom.

"What's going on here? I swear..."

As the polar bear disciplines the pets, PanRoo comes home. She kicks her pointed toe pump heels off onto the floor, peels off her tight maroon sheath dress, throws on an oversized T-shirt, hops into the sunroom, takes LeDrun out of her pouch, places him on the windowsill and collapses in the swivel chair.

Sensing Pan's energy, everyone shuts up.

"Are you OK, Honeysuckle? How was the election? Would you like some tea?" asks Pol, taking the other swivel chair.

"I got it! Dragon Well tea is master Pan's favorite. Coming right up!" woofs BarKockalotte, wearing his red recovery goggles. The dog stands up and snatches Purrplexy.

"Fruck off!" Purrplexy yowls and air-scratches.

"I cannot see very well. You make sure I don't spill the hot tea." BarKockalotte carries the wiggling cat to the kitchen.

"You don't understand! My whiskers are compromised!" Cat screaming is heard from the kitchen.

***********

"For starters, I scuffed the front bumper of the car," says PanRoo, looking outside with empty eyes.

"You what?" Pol's raised voice reaches Pan's gloomy panda face and softens up.

"Don't worry, Pansy. I'll take care of the scuffing. And given the sore aura around you, you are an unelected HOA board member. Did Pilferine beat ya?" teases Polisco, putting his fat index finger in his right nostril, stirring it in a circle.

"Master Pan, here is your tea," purrs Purrplexy as she brings over a cup of tea.

"I made the tea single-pawedly!" barks BarKockalotte, preventing the cat from stealing his credit.

"No. The winner was Mr. Thorn, the little punk porcupines' dad across the street," grunts Pan, taking a sip of tea, spitting a tealeaf back into the cup, and placing it back on the coffee table.

"The garage band with a bullet-proof truck?" barks BarKockalotte. "I hate them! They threw a drum stick at me one time!"

"Bumpy! Bumpy!" coos Joecub, leaning against the dog, face puckering up.

"Like father, like sons..." growls Polisco with a disgusted face.

"It all started with the arrest scene," narrates PanRoo. "This morning, I got myself ready in the car for the HOA election. But when I opened the garage door, I saw two police cars parking in front of the porcupines' house. Two cops were handcuffing the chubbiest porcupine with purple-dyed quills. I just wanted to leave the disturbing scene for the board election a.s.a.p. As I was backing out of the garage while observing the arrest scene in the rear-view mirror, somehow, I overcorrected the steering wheel and scuffed the front bumper."

PanRoo grabs the teacup off the table. She purses her lips and blows the tealeaves on the hot tea surface like a pouted rotating searchlight.

"It is not your fault, master Pan!" woofs BarKockalotte.

"The self-driving car is not reliable, and the garage door is too narrow. Whoever designed it should be shot. And don't worry. Master Pol can always fix the scuffing with some rubbing compound. He can fix everything!" The dog gives the masters a tongue-hanging grin.

"You need some rubbing compound for your brown nose," scorns Purrplexy.

"No biggie. I can fix it. It is not the first time and surely won't be the last," grumbles Polisco.

He grabs Purrplexy off the floor to pet for alleviating the distress from the thought of the scuffed car.

The cat, however, repulsed by Pol's booger fingers, tries to dig her claws into a table leg for resistance, but misses the target table leg over and over again. She gives in after a brief struggle.

Polisco strokes the pouty squirmy cat contently.

"No biggie?" Pan raises her bitter voice. "Those white marks are like attack ads against my own campaign. They made me lose the election!" frowns and growls the unelected HOA board member.

"I am sure the scuffing marks took full responsibility for your loss," chaffs Polisco, gazing intensely at a booger on the tip of his fingers, which has been freshly excavated out of his nostril.

"You don't understand! Getting the HOA board membership fulfills the mandatory community credits in school. All teachers have to do it. And I've done everything to ensure the win!" admits PanRoo.

"As far as I know, you've done some quite dirty stuff to ensure the win, Honeysuckle." Polisco rolls a booger into a tiny ball with his two fingers.

# 24

# Universal Language

In the sunroom, Polisco sits in the swivel chair, crafting a booger into a perfect ball with his two stubby fingertips. Purrplexy, sitting on Pol's thighs, is nervously watching the noxious rolling ball, fearing that he might smear it on her fur, like what the dog did to her with LeDrun's wee recently.

"Why don't you share all your dirty campaign moves, my sweet Sore?" The polar bear makes an "L" on his forehead.

"How dare you?" reproaches PanRoo. "I've done everything I could, and they are not dirty moves! You see these pointed toe heels? They feel like a pair of pliers clamped onto my round feet, but they look elegant. Same idea with the tight sheath dress. Hard to breathe in it, but it highlights my professionalism and curvy body figure. Two birds with one stone. I surely thought I could win some male members' votes with the...anyway," PanRoo glances at the Polisco and bites her tongue.

"To ensure the win this year, I've befriended all of the board members, every single one of them!" continues the sore and bitter Pan.

"Mr. Jack the donkey likes yodeling, so I hired a vocal coach and joined his 'The Yodeling Ass' club. Mr. Billy the goat loves headbutt wresting, so I wrestled with him in the park and suffered a mild concussion. Ms. Woo the wombat is enthused about herbivore poop recycling for renewable energy, so I saved all mine... I even molded them into little cubes for the sake of connecting with the wombat lady..." PanRoo reveals her campaign strategies.

"What about the dirty stuff you did to your campaign rivals?" questions Polisco.

"They are all legit campaign moves to disqualify them," justifies PanRoo, "namely, Pilferine the raccoon from next door and Thorn the porcupine from across the street. In order to beat them, I initiated the neighborhood scuttlebutt: Pilferine got the Virus from her late husband; Thorn is a senile crook and a child molester; the two sleep together according to multiple anonymous witnesses...Hell, I even made a couple of phone calls to the police to report on the punk porcupines' juniors..." confesses the panda kangaroo, totally forgetting about the cup of tea held in her paws.

"Daddy Police!" cheers Joecub, clapping his tiny bear paws.

"So you made a deal with the devil for the bogus HOA? What planet are you from?" reproaches the polar bear.

"Moon Sticks. Thank you for reminding me," PanRoo's round face dims down.

"The only two teachers in school who still haven't fulfilled the community credits are me and Mr. Charlie the elephant immigrant from Moon Bonbon. That's the real reason they didn't elect me. That and the scuffed car bumper," murmurs Pan, the legal alien.

"You don't dream very high, do ya?" Pol shakes his head, rolling and squeezing the booger ball in his fingers.

"What high dreams justify low deeds?" LeDrun slowly utters

the question from upon the windowsill. The death messenger then chants:

**Lonely stars**

**Wholly cosmos**

**Multitude colors and forms**

**One brilliant existence**

**Unique Essence**

**Universal Language**

"Hey! Stop mumbling nonsense! Did you know all the crazy stuff she did? Why didn't you help? You useless Wenis Head!" Polisco blames LeDrun. He aims at the tortoise and then flicks the booger bomb towards him.

Purrplexy's round cat eyes attentively trace the trajectory of Pol's booger bomb ejected from his fingers as it dives right into PanRoo's cup of tea.

Polisco, the guilty polar bear, places his right paw on his pursed lips.

"I just saw a fruit fly. You guys have got to remember to close the sunroom door!" growls Pan, protruding her lips to meet the teacup halfway for a sip.

"Eww, the new Dragon Well tea tastes weird," Pan, the unaware booger tea victim, sniffs her tea and smacks her lips.

"Honey, no need to stress over anything. Let me warm up your tea for you," solaces the culpable polar bear.

Polisco snatches Pan's booger tea and scuttles away.

The liberated cat immediately jumps toward the windowsill but only bangs her head on the edge, thanks to the neck cone.

\*\*\*\*\*\*\*\*\*\*\*

"Remember the Origin, the ball of goo?" sighs LeDrun on the windowsill. "Each soon-to-be-born baby is endowed with unique Essence but also charged with two Magic Powers: Love and Fear. It is Mother Nature's intricate design: Essence is unique whereas Love and Fear are universal. The universality of Love and Fear can relay what's INSIDE you and communicate with the OUTSIDE world. In other words, Love and Fear speak the **Universal Language**."

"What Universal Language?" asks PanRoo in doubt. "I had to learn the F language that's spoken on Planet **F**. It's not my mother tongue. That's why I have an accent. It's part of the reason they didn't elect me."

"The Universal Language transcends nationalities and cultures," explains LeDrun. "It's a language of your *essential motivations*. Love may charge your Energy to radiate multiple colors; Fear may charge your Energy to form various weapons. It doesn't matter,because the world around you will intuitively know whether what say and do are charged by Love or by Fear. Unique Essence makes one distinct from another with particular traits and talents; Universal Language speaks to each other as one race. The diversity of Essence enriches the world; the universality of Love and Fear unites us as One," enlightens LeDrun, standing up on the windowsill.

"Bogus," meows Purrplexy under the windowsill. "So without fPhones and words, we can communicate with each other? That's nuts! I'm starting to suspect that you bamboozled us into offering you free accommodations."

"Brr-haha!" laughs the death messenger. "Words and communication technologies are often redundant and, in many cases, manipulative and deceptive, on the self-discovery journey. Instead, Love-charged Energy and/or Fear-charged Energy serve as essential signals for you to communicate and interact with the outside world: the interplay of Love Energy between yours and others' reflects your Essence; the vigilant Fear Energy protects you by understanding the contextual environments. There are no language barriers or lies in Love and Fear communication. You intuitively get the essential message sent off by others." LeDrun snaps his fingers in the air.

"Like you go to a party, and you intuitively know who's into you and who's not? Who's sincere and who's pretentious?" woofs BarKockalotte on the floor.

"That's hilarious. Nobody is into you," mocks Purrplexy under the windowsill.

"I think it's more like sending a text message, but only with your Love or Fear Energy," figures Purrplexy. "You are the phone, and your Love/Fear Energy carries the texts…and emoji stuff."

"Do you know anything else besides texting?" BarKockalotte barks off his disapproval.

"I know sexting, too!" defies Purrplexy proudly.

"Shush, you two!" PanRoo growls at the pets. "If Love and Fear speak a language deemed essential and universal, how come I don't know? I don't discern hidden Love or Fear signals embedded in communication."

"Yes you know," rectifies LeDrun. "You were born with it."

LeDrun then levitates above the windowsill and chants:

*Love wants to play. Fear stays away.*
*Love draws in. Fear pushes out.*
*Love participates. Fear avoids.*
*Love includes. Fear excludes.*
*Love engages. Fear detaches.*

*Love desires. Fear prevents.*
*Love ventures. Fear secures.*
*Love ATTRACTS. Fear REPELS.*

# 25

# Love Attracts, Fear Repels

"I knew it!" claims Polisco, returning with a new cup of tea.

"Here is your tea, Suckle. Nice and warm." Polisco puts down the teacup on the table and slouches in the swivel chair.

"Sack Neck," says the polar bear to the tortoise, "the Love attracts Fear repels shit you just raved about, I knew you could pull off some tricks like that. So why have you not already used your magic to repel all Pansy's rivals and thus help her get elected? Chant all you want as long as you make yourself useful!"

"I've never thought of that. Could you repel all my rivals, LeDrun?" inquires PanRoo with hope.

LeDrun descends from the air and sits back down onto the windowsill. The disturbed death messenger frowns and exhales.

"You don't understand," articulates the magic tortoise. "The **'Love attracts Fear repels'** is the essential way of interaction. When two living beings encounter each other, their Love- or Fear-charged Energy fields exchange essential communicative signals. If you have ever held two magnets in your paws, you know what attraction and repulsion feel like."

"I know!" BarKockalotte raises his paws, wearing red goggles. "I have played magnet balls! With basic rules of attraction and repulsion, they can form all sorts of shapes: cubes, orbs, parallel lines..."

"I've played real ones!" The competitive cat raises her paw.

"Quiet!" LeDrun scolds the pets. "Not exactly the same as magnets with fixed polarities, either Love or Fear, not both at the same time, will charge your Energy to send out signals. That being said, when interacting with the world, YOU are the one who decides whether to concentrate your Energy to attract, or focus your Energy to repel."

"So I can form and reverse Energy fields by switching the charges?" barks BarKockalotte. "That's insane! I would be totally perplexed like the cat!"

"Purrplexy cat!" coos Joecub, pulling on the cat's green neck cone to play tug of war.

"Hey! Purrplexy is a stage name and I love it!" hisses Purrplexy at the dog, wriggling and wiggling her head to resist the cub.

"For instance," continues LeDrun, ignoring the commotion of the pets and cub.

"When you are interested in someone or something, your Love charges up your Energy for further interaction. Like a magnetic field, your Love Energy forms an Energy field that everyone around you can perceive, because Love speaks the **Universal Language**. Words are often redundant, but they help you radiate in multiple colors. Similarly, when you are not interested in someone or something, your Energy carries Fear warnings naturally designed to repel. Like a Love-charged Energy field, a Fear-charged Energy field can be perceived by others nearby, because Fear also speaks the **Universal Language**. Words and social performances are sometimes employed in various forms to cover up Fear messages. Nonetheless, you need to be mindful. What Energy do you send out to the world? Is it out of Love or out of Fear?" smiles LeDrun, guzzling the elixir from the crystal flask with contentment.

"That's too much to digest," woofs BarKockalotte. "Could you sing the Love Attracts Fear Repels song one more time? I need to take notes." The dog gets his notebook ready.

"Absolutely!" LeDrun beams from upon the windowsill. He stows his flask inside his shell and levitates in the air. The death messenger's body glitters in a purple aura. He hovers around the animals and sings like a loud buzzing purple beetle:

> *Love wants to play. Fear stays away.*
> *Love draws in. Fear pushes out.*
> *Love participates. Fear avoids.*
> *Love includes. Fear excludes.*
> *Love engages. Fear detaches.*
> *Love desires. Fear prevents.*
> *Love ventures. Fear secures.*
> *Love ATTRACTS. Fear REPELS.*

"That doesn't add up," PanRoo shakes her round head in the swivel chair.

\*\*\*\*\*\*\*\*\*\*\*

"You said 'Love wants to play,'" PanRoo air quotes. "I want to join the HOA to make the neighborhood a better place. That's Love, right? How come my 'Love message,'" Pan rolls her eyes, "did not attract the majority of votes?"

"Say whatever you want, but what you did for winning the HOA seat had nothing to do with Love," clarifies LeDrun, landing back on the windowsill. "**Love desires an interactive experience by engag-**

*ing; **Fear secures a certain goal by preventing**.* The Energy you spent in securing the majority votes was charged by Fear, the Fear of loss: yodeling with the ass, headbutting the goat, poop molding for the wombat, slandering other candidates... all Fear Energy. I'm not surprised that the HOA board didn't vote for you. Fear REPELS."

"Not true! They didn't choose me because I am not originally from here. I'm an outsider!" argues PanRoo.

"Remember the Fear excursion in my big **D** Lair?" asks LeDrun, pacing on the windowsill.

"How could we forget? It blinded me, almost!" barks BarKockalotte, pointing to his red recovery goggles.

"Blind most!" Joecub comforts the dog.

"Yeah. I went through the Death Portal and found myself among a clan of hyenas. I was scared, especially because they all laughed at me together," recollects and admits the panda kangaroo.

"Then your Fear bubble projected an image of a hyena all around you in order to fit in, right?" nurtures LeDrun.

"That's my camouflage," defends Pan. "You said our Fear bubble is versatile in various forms. It could toughen us up to deter impending danger, or disguise us to blend in, or detach from a harmful relationship, or block the surroundings to avoid pain, or...they are all OK because we do what we have to do for self-protection."

"Of course they are," replies LeDrun. "They are all forms of your intrinsic Guard. But Pan, **Guard is for self-protection, not for making connection.** When you camouflaged yourself as a yodeler, a headbutt wrestler, or a cubic poop recycler, others could perceive your inflated Fear bubble and could receive your Fear-charged Energy because Fear is the Universal Language."

PanRoo pouts in the chair, silently organizing words to refute LeDrun's remarks.

"How do we know exactly?" woofs BarKockalotte, lying on his front paws. "I mean, I bark a lot. Is my barking out of Love or Fear? How about howling?"

"Oh! I hate your howling," chatters Purrplexy from the windowsill. "Whenever you chin up and howl, I simply wish I could fly above your big mouth and pee in it.

"***Love wants to play. Fear stays away....***" LeDrun begins humming his "Love Attracts Fear Repels" song again.

"I disagree." The postured PanRoo interrupts the chanting tortoise.

"I yodeled with Mr. Jack in order to bond with him. And you were saying I did that out of Fear? You cannot just press charges against me without evidence. I love yodeling!" Pan raises her double chin and glares at the death messenger.

"Nah. I was with you the whole time," LeDrun shakes his bulbous head.

"Love charges your Energy for engaging in an *interactive experience* that brings *joy* and *fulfillment*; Fear summons your Energy for *repulsing* someone or something that imposes immediate or potential *pain or danger*. When the interplay is out of Love, your Energy emanates joy and the desire of continuity; when the expression is out of Fear, your Energy gives off a vibe of unease and defensiveness. Remember when you camouflaged as a hyena, how stressed you were and how strongly you hoped to break away? Did you feel the same when you were yodeling with Mr. Jackass?" LeDrun yodels and kicks in the air.

"I enjoyed the yodeling! And the headbutt wrestling! And poop recycling!" shouts Pan in denial.

"**Your words often deceive, but the Universal Language never lies.** When you fake it, others intuitively know it no matter how well you disguise it. Your Fear Energy texts honest communicative messages to others. And by nature, they immediately understand whether you are genuinely interested or, to put it eloquently, FULL OF IT." The tortoise levitates and wave dances over to the self-deceptive panda kangaroo.

Pan flies into a rage out of humiliation. She suddenly hops up and seizes the dancing tortoise out of the air.

"Ouch! Son of a female..." the dog growls as PanRoo accidentally steps on his tail. He turns his head around and shows his teeth. Through his goggles, he realizes that it was Pan. He whines and whimpers: "Sorry, master Pan, that was my Fear Energy..."

"Why didn't you tell me earlier? You were in my pouch the whole time!" PanRoo shakes LeDrun, holding him in her right paw as if she were shaking a tortoiseshell dice container.

"You have to go through the pain for deep reflection." LeDrun struggles to breathe.

PanRoo is deflated. She puts the tortoise back on the windowsill, head hanging down.

"Plus, do you have any idea how much fun it was to watch a panda bear yodeling?" giggles and yodels the impish death messenger.

"Sleep on the windowsill tonight! No pouch for you! You exploited my Fear energy!" yells PanRoo.

A transparent, membrane-like Fear bubble inflates around the puppy-eyed tortoise.

"Brahahahaha!" Polisco laughs at LeDrun. "Finally, you got what you deserve. Exploit Pan's Fear Energy... try ME, Wenis Head! Oh! Sorry! I don't have any Fear!"

"Really?" LeDrun raises his right eyebrow from inside the bubble. "Why did you want to change Pan's tea exactly?"

"Ladies and gentlemen, the booger bomb tea!" reveals Purrplexy from under the windowsill.

She sticks one paw out and snaps it in the air like shooting a free throw.

"The what?!" roars PanRoo at the petrified polar bear.

# 26

## Hyenas' Laugh

It's late afternoon. The pets and the cub play in the backyard. PanRoo curls up alone on the couch in the living room. The TV is on. Her vitality is off.

The bear couple has gone through a rough patch on their already bumpy conjugal journey. PanRoo claims that her failed election was due to Polisco's flagrant lack of support. In Polisco's defense, an HOA is a fake community, and the whole campaign for its board membership is half-witted. With one accusation piling upon another during their fights, the couple lists off all the things they think they have been wronged by the other since their first date. Hitherto, Polisco's booger bomb in PanRoo's Dragon Well tea has given her a one-point lead.

"Wonderland! Wonderland!" a seductive voice comes from the master bedroom.

"Wonderland" is the polar bear's secret code for his round and fluffy rear end.

Turning the TV's volume up, PanRoo unenthusiastically drags her feet into the bedroom and closes the door.

Polisco buries his head in the pillow, using his elbows and knees as a scaffold to elevate his fluffy bear butt in the air. Pan's entrance into the room instantly recharges the heavenward ass. It twerks and bounces aloft, beckoning the panda kangaroo for a wild ride.

"Tender and juicy, a burst of flavor!" Pol enhances his rear end, marketing endeavors as Pan approaches him.

"You mean the pungent canyon?" teases PanRoo. She kneels down, grabs Pol's wonderland with both paws, and starts simulating.

"Oh! You are abusive! I am stretched! Butter!" the polar bear over actor jabbers from beneath to glorify the fanciful violator.

PanRoo is convulsed with laughter. She rolls off Polisco and lies next to him.

"How about I cede my wonderland as a truce?" proposes Polisco.

"Deal, under one condition," negotiates Pan, rolling away from Pol. "Give me an honest answer to why you didn't support my campaign."

"I'm ready for a second round! You are so addictive!" Polisco avoids PanRoo's question. He faces down and elevates his wonderland to a new height.

"Don't deflect the question!" Pan grabs the elastic waistband of Pol's shorts and yanks it towards her.

The polar bear wobbles a little and then falls over Pan's side.

"Ok," Pol acquiesces, scratching Pan's back.

"Initially, I couldn't put my finger on it. But I had a hunch that you didn't enjoy the whole campaign circus. I knew how frustrated you were when you couldn't yodel, and how guilty you felt after you called the police to report on Mr. Thorn's sons. The other day, LeDrun said Love and Fear is the Universal Language. It actually gave my hunch an explanation. The Fear-charged Energy you sent off during campaigning was received by both the voters and me. That's why I stayed out of it. And..." hesitates Polisco.

"Honest answer?" asks Polisco.

"Honest answer," confirms PanRoo.

"I feel repulsed by your camouflage because that's not the panda kangaroo I love," admits Polisco.

"Remember when I saw you among those hyenas? Granted you were scared among the clan, but was camouflaging your only way to stay safe? And how long did you plan to stay disguised as a hyena? Because as far as I know, you are an adorable panda kangaroo, not a hideous...Anyway, my point is: you are not the one I fell in love with when you camouflage, but you seem to do it a lot. To be brutally honest, you are never yourself when you are around others: your students, coworkers, friends as well as those in my family and social circles... When you are with hyenas, you laugh; with asses, you yodel; with goats, you headbutt; with wombats, you mold turds; even with me..." Polisco bites his tongue.

"With you? What about me with you?" Pan turns her fluffy head towards Pol, frowning.

"You camouflage around me sometimes. For example, when you watch snowball games with me, I look at a roaring and swearing panda kangaroo, knowing that it's not you. Because deep down, I am aware that you don't really enjoy snowball games. In the past, I just knew that you were insincere. Now, according to the Bulbous Head, you might be just in Fear." Polisco looks into PanRoo's eyes.

Red and watery, PanRoo's eyeballs roll aside to avoid direct contact with Pol's. She exhales heavily.

"I knew that," confesses PanRoo. "I've been contemplating ever since LeDrun said Love and Fear are the Universal Language that reveals essential motivations and communicates true intentions. I feel like a clown in that everyone can actually receive my Fear Energy through my camouflage. What's the whole point of camouflaging anyway? Maybe that's how I repel others. That's why I don't have any close friends. And the last thing I want to do is to push you away. But I don't know why I habitually camouflage. And the very thought that kills me is that: who am I in disguise? Who am I at all?" ponders the panda kangaroo. She looks out the window, eyes empty.

"If you habitually camouflage, you must have never felt safe around others. Why? You know I'll always protect you," Polisco tabs his thumb on Pan's forehead accompanied with a tongue click to imitate her coveted male part.

"It's the laugh." Pan rolls over. "It haunts me. Whenever I am with others, I hear the laugh. Thus, I avoid being targeted by becoming invisible in camouflage. Because I hide myself so readily and for so long, I don't know who I really am."

"What laugh? The hyenas' laugh?" Polisco is confused. "Pancakes, it's not your fault. It's those ugly hyenas' laugh that triggered your Fear bubble," Pol raises his chin and opens his mouth to imitate the laugh of the hyenas.

Through the bedroom window fissures, BarKockalotte's howling from the backyard elbows in to join Pol's distorted hyena howling.

"I want to know who I am. And I need Love," Pan groans in pain.

"Well, maybe you sense their Fear Energy first so that you have to respond by putting on your own camouflage," consults Pol. "Didn't the hyenas laugh at you first before your Fear bubble projected you into a hyena? Your students, colleagues, fake friends, my family members and buddies, total strangers, and whatnot may as well send off their Fear Energy to you first. Do you receive Love Energy from your students and colleagues? How about other animals in town?"

"Of course not," PanRoo's face puckers up and then satires: "It's a real lovefest, isn't it? Who sends off the Fear Energy first? Me or others? The chicken or the egg?"

"You forgot the most important thing," Pol begins to lose his patience as he finds Pan's depressing energy contagious. "You have a loving family. Me, the cub, even the useless pets love you."

"Oh! Family!" Pan raises her bitter voice. "My mom didn't share much of her Love Energy with me. I had to disguise who I truly was and perform the role of a perfect girl in her eyes. And ever since I became a mother, the Fear has been doubled! I need to protect the cub from so much...and you don't help much!"

PanRoo's indiscriminate shooting makes Pol realize that he has opened Pandora's box by mentioning the family. He quickly jumps off the bed.

"I cannot help you if you start attacking me again, Honeysuckle. You need to talk to a shrink! Watch!" growls Pol, standing next to the bed.

He swiftly strips himself and jumps around like a cheerleader doing disco fingers: "Milk! Milk! Lemonade!"

"You know I cannot resist that..." Pan lights up and places her double chin on the edge of bed for better view of the stage.

Pol turns around and bends over, peaking through his butt cheeks, and talks to Pan through his crouch:

"Maybe you want to consult Dr. Phinkster?" the polar bear contracts and relaxes Dr. Phinkster to demonstrate his deep expertise.

"Eww! Get a room!" LeDrun suddenly appears from nowhere, startling the passionate performer on stage.

"What the fruck!" roars Polisco. "We are in our room! Get the fruck out! You old pervert!"

"Calm down, Gee!" LeDrun enunciates slowly. "I have no interest in your bear privates. Put on your swimming suit and meet me by the poolside. We need to take care of Pan's self-confusion."

The death messenger floats away, only to stick his head back in through the door crack:

"How did you get it to flap around so exuberantly?" sniggers the tortoise.

"I swear!" growls the embarrassed polar bear.

# 27

## Fear Charged

It is a mackerel sky. Wavy white clouds spread out like scales on an infinite ocean-blue fish. BarKockalotte wears his red goggles, paddling around in the sparkly swimming pool to escort Joecub, who rides an inflatable yellow duck. Purrplexy lounges under a cantilever umbrella. Her large green neck cone and cat-eye sunglasses fashion her into a cool cat lamp. Next to the chaise lounge rests LeDrun. Eyes closed, the magic tortoise uses his shell as a rocking chair, leisurely oscillating back and forth on the hardwood pool deck.

With a cracking sound, the sunroom door is opened. PanRoo and Polisco join the animalistic pool party.

"What's up, Old Perv?" grunts Pol to LeDrun. He "accidentally" kicks the tortoiseshell and effectively sets it in motion like a spinning top.

"Master Pol! I heard your howling in your bedroom earlier! I bonded with you! Did you hear mine?" grins BarKockalotte, pushing his goggles up on his forehead.

"That was not howling. Watch out! Bear down!" roars the polar bear, splashing into the swimming pool.

PanRoo picks up the twirling tortoise and places the giddy death messenger on the rattan coffee table. She then occupies the lounger and puts the pouty cat lamp on her belly.

"So, you said I have what?" inquires Pan, looking at the disoriented tortoise.

"Hang on a sec," moans LeDrun, breaking a crystal flask out of his shell and guzzling up. "I need to suppress the nausea."

**"Inner struggle is the worst war; self-confusion is the ultimate loss**," burps LeDrun. "As you said in the bedroom, you don't know who you are."

"Right, as if everyone else knew," PanRoo rolls her eyes. "Ask the kitten if she knows who she is," Pan challenges.

"Well, I am nobody now," meows Purrplexy on Pan's round tummy. "But after I rise to stardom, everyone will know who I am!"

"**Know thyself and be known, the art of Love,**" a tipsy smile blooms on LeDrun's wrinkly face. "Upon being born from the Origin, nobody knows who you are, not your parents, nor yourself. However, your Essence is already within you. It's embedded in every single thought and feeling you perceive INSIDE. Interacting with the world, you develop infinite thoughts and feelings. It is your Essence vibrating inside you, up and down like ocean waves. Most of them are **flashy and transient**. You don't really act upon all of them and just let them be."

"Like those unspeakable thoughts that flash through a tomcat's mind when he sees a hot pussy cat like me," purrs Purrplexy, cleansing on Pan's round belly.

"Puss..." Before Joecub finishes the word, BarKockalotte covers his mouth while leering at the cat.

"Anywho," LeDrun continues, "at certain essential moments, the **waves of your Essence resonate so intensely** that you are compelled to action. In such cases, you will need to concentrate your Energy on what you are about to say or do. In other words, when interacting with the world, you follow your Essence and use your Energy. And between your Essence and Energy is Love and Fear, the essential Guide and Guard. By interpreting the waves of your Essence, either Love or Fear will charge your Energy into actions. Fear-charged actions repel certain situations or interactions for the sake of safety. Love-charged actions engage in interactive experiences that will attract your Essential Observers." LeDrun beams contently and resumes suckling from his crystal flask.

"So when camouflaging..." ponders PanRoo.

"Oh!" LeDrun interrupts her. "One more thing: when you charge your Energy for taking actions, it is **either Love-charged or Fear-charged**, never simultaneously. Like you cannot inhale and exhale at the same time, nor have a concurrent ebb and flow..."

"Don't listen to his gobbledygook!" growls Polisco from the pool. "No Fear needed. I'll protect you!" the polar bear flexes his biceps in the water.

"I'll protect you too, master Pan!" howls BarKockalotte in goggles.

"Ugh! Wash your nose!" yowls Purrplexy at the dog.

Upon request, Joecub, on the inflatable duck, scoops up some pool water in his tiny paws and pours it carefully onto the dog's nose.

"Figure of speech, buddy!" Mr. Bar shakes off the nose water violently. The goggles fall off his forehead and into the pool, buoying up and down with the waves like a miniature red bra.

"Is that so? I challenge you to stay underwater and sing your favorite song simultaneously!" squeals LeDrun at the polar bear.

"Challenge accepted!" roars the competitive polar bear, submerging into the pool.

"But he cannot..." worries Pan on the lounging chair.

"Nah, he's stubborn but not stupid. I just want to shut him up for a second," winks LeDrun.

"Ok," frowns PanRoo. "The resonance of Essence, vibration or waves, whatever is coming from inside, how do I know whether it's Love or Fear? I must be feeling it as Fear most of the time because I camouflaged habitually..."

"Good question," the tortoise clears his throat. "You know it's Love when you want that experience to happen and continue; you know it's Fear when you stay away from it or want it to end ASAP.

When your action and interaction are infused with Love-charged Energy:

*1. you feel joy and fulfillment but not the lapse of time;*

*2. you learn about the unique traits and talents you possess through your own experience and others' recognition;*

*3. you feel invigorated and energized;*

*4. you long for the continuity of the experience;*

*5. you inspire others and are enriched by others in kind through the interplay of Love energy;.*

*6. you cherish all the experiences and memories and use them to know thyself and be known.*

When your action and interaction are infused with Fear-charged Energy:

*1. you feel anxiety or agony;*

*2. you know you would instead prefer the experience of some-*

*thing or someone else, but you justify what you do out of necessity;*

*3. you long for the experience to end as soon as possible, thus time becomes pressing;*

*4. you feel depleted or exhausted afterwards;*

*5. you block and exclude others so that you can be safe or feel secure;*

*6. you try to numb the experiences or bury the memories.*

\*\*\*\*\*\*\*\*\*\*\*

"Did you guys hear me singing underwater?" Polisco suddenly resurfaces from his dive, water dripping off his white, matted fur. He stands at the edge of the pool with BarKockalotte's red goggles in his right paw, aiming at the tortoise.

"Nope. Noisy LeDrun jibbers the whole time," complains Purrplexy.

"Well, I couldn't sing underwater," the polar bear shrugs. "I am a polar bear, not a bowhead whale. But I found the goggles...Wenis Head! Don't move!" Polisco waves the goggles at the targeted tortoise.

LeDrun swiftly jumps onto PanRoo's pouch and uses the cat as his bunker.

"A cat bunker? It doesn't work!" jeers Pol, throwing the pair of goggles out of the pool.

Purrplexy's large green neck cone catches the dog's goggles like a magnetic baseball mitt.

"Master Pol, my goggles..." BarKockalotte pushes the cub aside on the inflatable duck and paddles to the edge of the pool.

"So if I do most things out of Fear," says PanRoo to LeDrun on her belly, "I'm doomed to bury the majority of my life in the sandbox and toss it away...as if I've never lived?" sighs the panda kangaroo, eyes dimmed down.

"Naturally," LeDrun shakes his head. "Love or Fear charges your Energy in harmonious waves, and dances with the world in beautiful equilibrium," LeDrun swings and shakes his body. "No wholesome and robust life spends the majority of their Energy out of Fear. The organic balance of Love and Fear is broken for one reason. Remember the hyenas' laugh in your head? It's the Virus," reveals the death messenger.

"I'm out of here!" Purrplexy bounces up and jumps off PanRoo's belly.

BarKockalotte seizes the moment to grab the cat's neck cone and drags her towards the pool to retain his goggles. The resisting cat desperately pulls her body back but loses the tug of war due to the disparity between their weight classes.

"She doesn't have the Virus!" Pol denies for Pan.

"Yes. She does," confirms the death messenger. He slips into Pan's pouch and looks up into the mackerel sky. "But I'll save her and everybody else in the family, just like how you saved me."

"Do it fast, please!" whines BarKockalotte. "I don't want master Pan to kill herself! I won't allow it!" weeps the dog, mourning his late master.

"It's time to tell you the truth," reveals LeDrun. "I'm under investigation. To be accurate, the whole death department is under an internal investigation for neglect of duty by the Natural Law Office. They claim that we have missed a colossal number of death cases on Planet **F**. You've all been to my work lair. Death messengers first receive death signals sent by someone's Fear Energy. You know, the purple lightening-like signals you saw. Then we follow the signal back to the sender through the Death Portal. Next, we extract the Essence out of the corpse and return it to the Origin. The Law of Nature designs everything flawlessly. We've never missed a death until the Virus came into the picture and messed up the organic system. Well, at least I blame the Virus. So, out of curiosity, I began my own secret investigation a while ago, and in fact, collected some really fascinating evidence. It's time to bring you all in on my secret project. We have a chance to beat the Virus together."

"I don't know," PanRoo shakes her fluffy head. "It sounds like a dangerous mission. Look what happened to you! You almost got killed! Could you ask your fellow death messengers instead?"

"Nah," LeDrun shakes his wrinkly head. "Death messengers are Fear experts. They know everything about Fear, but little about Love. I need those who are curious about the world. And curiosity is the color of Love."

"Why are YOU so special?" woofs BarKockalotte.

LeDrun takes out the crystal flask from inside his shell. He guzzles and burps: "I've got this. And what have you all got to lose? You're all infected anyway."

"I'm not infected nor am I interested!" rejects Polisco, holding a grudge against LeDrun for the humiliation in the bedroom and the pool.

Silence.

"I am curious. Count me in!" meows Purrplexy, recalling her traumatic fall from the sky in the **I** Resort.

"Me too!" barks BarKockalotte, recollecting his terrifying police encounter in the **D** Lair.

"Me three!" Joecub shows off his math as usual.

"Fine. Let's do it." PanRoo joins the team, introspecting her HOA campaign farce and more.

"Where did you store all the evidence?" woofs BarKockalotte.

"Over there, in a cloud," LeDrun points up to the mackerel sky.

# 28

# Shapeshifting

It's a Sunday morning. A big fly clumsily flies and buzzes around in the family's living room. Hearing the noise, Polisco rushes out of the bedroom into the laundry room and gets the electric fly swatter off the wall. When he returns, the fly has simply disappeared.

"Oh, you are smart! You know how much I enjoy the crackling sound with miniature fireworks when I roast you with this baby!" Polisco roars, holding the electric swatter and circling around the room in search of the fly.

"Stop looking. That was me," says LeDrun on the bay windowsill in the sunroom, meditating with legs crossed.

"Are you serious? You can turn into a fly? Do it again! I want to see!" Polisco acclaims, waving the swatter in his paw.

"Yes. And it's called shapeshifting. All death messengers can do it," confirms the magic tortoise.

"So, you can turn into whatever you want, or just insects?" Polisco is intrigued. He quickly checks in the direction of the bedroom and whispers to LeDrun: "How about a hot lady bear with NICE, you know…" the polar bear draws two half circles on his protruding chest.

"Brahaha!" LeDrun laughs. "I don't know. I haven't done it since I was wounded, so it gets a little rusty. This morning, I turned into a fly to test it out. I could only shapeshift my body, but my head remained a tortoise. After bumping my head on the window several times as I navigated with my new wings, I now have to regain my orientation. I'm almost ready for the day trip with you today."

"Hahaha! Wait, what do you mean the day trip with me?" Pol is amused but confused.

"You are going to the Barnyard of Commerce brunch event, right? I'm going with you to sneak in. A buddy's day trip." LeDrun clicks his tongue and winks from the windowsill.

"How do you know? Honestly, I wouldn't entertain the idea of you buzzing around me during my brunch." Polisco frowns with zero enthusiasm.

"I'll definitely buzz around you like an insect until you agree to check my secret place in the clouds." The death messenger smiles graciously.

"Oh man. Could you just leave me alone?" Pol rolls his eyes. "It's not like your secret place is the Sanctuary. I have zero interest, OK? I'd better go take a shower," grumbles Pol in an unenthusiastic voice as he walks back to the master bedroom.

"Hmmm, I think I CAN shapeshift into a voluptuous lady bear," LeDrun murmurs.

"Really?" Polisco sticks his head out from behind the bedroom door with eyes lit up like two car headlights on high beam.

*******************

In the master bathroom, Polisco is taking a shower while PanRoo is curling and styling her fur in front of the mirror.

"Are you sure you don't want to save some water and shower with a bear friend?" Pol invites Pan from inside the steamy walk-in shower.

"No, thank you," declines Pan, looking in the mirror with a curling wand in her paw.

"But I have something special to offer!" Pol puts his face against the glass door, showing his lustful eyes and white teeth.

"Oh? Show me what you've got," grunts Pan, turning her head to give Pol her attention.

"I present a bouquet to my beautiful panda bride!" Pol grins, taking his face off the glass, turning around, widely spreading his buns, and pressing them hard against the shower glass.

"Ahaha! I like pink and white." Pan is amused. She holds out the curling wand, approaches the floral imprint on the glass, and pokes it with the metal rod.

"Oww! You are abusive!" Feeling the vibration through the shower glass, Pol retracts his ass.

"There's a yellow stain on the glass now, and I am not cleaning it." Pan points to the spot where Pol's bouquet made an impact earlier.

"Good morning!" A big fly with a mini tortoise head buzzes in.

"Ahh! A bee! No! A beetle! A talking beetle! Spray! Swatter! Pol!" PanRoo screams.

"Chill. That's LeDrun practicing his half-assed shapeshifting skills. Among all the amazing things in the world, he has to be a fly," grumbles Polisco, shaking his matted head in the shower.

"What amazing things? You mean like a hot lad..." hums the tortoise-headed fly.

"Fly is good! Fly is good!" Polisco immediately shuts LeDrun up and waves him off.

LeDrun sniggers and buzzes his way out, bumping his head on the doorframe.

He stumbles into the sunroom and lands right on the tip of Purrplexy's nose.

"Good morning!" LeDrun greets and grins, fluttering his wings against the cat's nose.

"Ahhh---meow---uuuu!" Purrplexy yowls and passes out.

"Oops." LeDrun flees the crime scene.

The moment he thrums out of the sunroom and into the backyard, Joecub points at him and laughs: "LeDrun fly! Hahahaha!"

"What? Where?" BarKockalotte halts his running and looks around.

"He come!" squeaks the cub.

The tortoise-headed fly crashes down onto the grass next to the cub and shifts his shape back into a tortoise.

"How did you know it was me?" moans and groans LeDrun, rubbing his bruised knee.

"Bulb head!" Joecub coos and giggles.

"I saw a large fly. It plummeted and disappeared near you," woofs the dog. He fanatically snuffles around the tortoise in search of the fallen fly.

"Quit sniffing!" reproaches LeDrun. "It was me!"

"No. I saw a fly." The dogged dog continues his search.

**Love in the knowing**

**Fear in the know**

**Ongoing exploration**

**Instant recognition**

"You didn't see a fly. You assumed one." The death messenger moans out his wisdom.

*********************

On the way to Polisco's networking brunch, LeDrun sits on the car dashboard like a tortoise bobblehead.

"I've never asked." LeDrun slowly opens his mouth. "Why are you going to the Barnyard of Commerce event? As far as I know, it's more for business owners than IT professionals," inquires the tortoise, bobbling his head.

"Because I've always wanted to have my own business," replies Polisco, one paw on the steering wheel and the other in his crouch. "And I hate my job."

"Do you?" LeDrun raises his brows.

"Who doesn't in this town?" Polisco grumbles and fondles. "We have become the slaves of our inventions. In restaurants and stores, there are customer service robots served by maintenance teams; in hospitals and clinics, there are diagnostic and operational robots served by staff teams; in schools, there are teaching robots served by admin teams, including PanRoo; security robots, public service robots, massage robots, adult entertaining robots…you name it! But you know what? With all these robots, nothing feels right. Nothing!" Polisco roars in frustration while flipping the bird to a sloth driver in the next lane.

"You kind of lapsed into whining and venting…" yawns the tortoise from up on the dashboard.

"Ok. Why do I hate my job? It's my boss, Hiporno. He is the biggest asshole on the planet," grunts Polisco with a disgusted face.

"Hiporno? It doesn't sound like a lofty name," sniggers LeDrun.

"Nah. Hiporno is a nickname we call him behind his back. The filthy rich hippopotamus asks us to address him as Sir Hippono as if he were a royal decedent or something. But we all know that his first bucket of gold came from an adult recreational film studio if you know what I mean. The name Hiporno is just more suitable for him. He is the number one most arrogant nickel poop in the world. I don't want to work for him. I want to be my own boss!" Polisco mutters with a hint of sour jealousy.

"You mean, nincompoop," rectifies LeDrun. "So, what is your genius business idea?"

"I want to develop subordinate robots. They are extremely agreeable and celebratory, no matter what you say or do. You can totally be the boss of them! There would be various models, and they would all come with lifetime update patch bundles..." Polisco's face lights up.

"I thought you hated robots..." LeDrun raises his eyebrows.

"Oh!" The passionate polar bear interrupts the tortoise. "You cannot sneak in as a fly. It just occurred to me that the Barnyard of Commerce event is sponsored by Croakina, a local pest control company owned by a bunch of fat frogs. You don't wanna become their snack, do ya?" Polisco reckons.

"Ummm. Good point. I normally like frogs, but not in the case that I am an insect. Fine. I do have a plan B for shapeshifting." LeDrun disappears on the last word.

"Hey! Where did you go?" The flustered polar bear shouts and looks around nervously.

"I am right here. Check in the mirror." The magic tortoise has transformed into a large, red, pus-saturated pimple on Polisco's nose.

"A pimple? What kind of shapeshifting school did you go to? It looks horrible on my nose!" Polisco growls into the mirror with anger and frustration.

"Chill. I meant to be a freckle, unnoticeable and harmless, only to possess the best location on your face to see everything you see. It's like sitting on the hood of a car while it's driving. But let me work on dwindling my size and color, all right? Don't scratch me because that will only irritate you," explains LeDrun with patience.

"You've irritated me already!" Polisco roars and growls in despair.

# 29

## Barnyard of Commerce

Located in an agritourist park, the Barnyard of Commerce Sunday brunch is the most attended business-networking event in town. Large golden bales of hay encircle a gentrified red wooden barn. It is the committee animals' office. Adjacent to the red barn erects a tall silver silo where the networking event is hosted.

After parking his car, Polisco sees Pilferine, the family's raccoon neighbor, at the entrance of the silo. The reception desk raccoon volunteer is busy greeting and giving out name bandages to the participants.

"Great." Polisco rolls his eyes as he approaches the entrance.

"Good morning, Mr. Police. What brought you here? Too bad it's a weapon-free zone. Otherwise, you could've shot some lights on the roof for recreation. You know what they say: like owners, like dogs," jeers Pilferine, holding a grudge against the neighbor for her roof light incident.

"Oh? Really," scorns Polisco at his good neighbor. "That explains why YOUR dog pisses and shits on our lawn."

The large pimple on the polar bear's nose sniggers.

Pilferine's face turns red. She hands a QR code badge sticker to

Polisco and stares at his red nose:

"Enjoy the brunch. I hope what's on your nose is not explosive!" The raccoon neighbor sends her best wishes.

"Damn it! LeDrun!" Polisco grunts in a muffled voice.

He places the sticker above his right nipular area and enters the silo.

***********

Sunbeams, through the dome glass top of the silo, cast down upon abundant food and drinks onto a circle of white tables and circumjacent blue balloons and golden hay rolls. Business animals are all dressed up, drinking and talking and laughing in pairs and clusters.

Polisco grabs a plate of seafood and a drink, jostles through the clamor and slouches against a large roll of hay. He looks up at the dome glass top and says to LeDrun:

"Pus Head, this place reminds me of your work lair. It's a phallic version of it. Look at the tip!"

"Why don't you go mingle?" asks LeDrun, ignoring Pol's comment.

"Nah. No rush. Background check first," says Polisco in a cocksure manner.

He puts down the food plate and takes out his fPhone. Turning on the scanner in the Barnyard of Commerce app, Polisco zooms the camera onto each animal's QR code sticker.

The scanner catches a peacock's code. A profile page pops up on Polisco's fPhone.

"Aha! An insurance agent," scorns Polisco. "Peacocks suck. First off, they steal the best name from all male species. Pee and cock!" Polisco raises his double chin toward the peacock.

"I don't think it's the same pee..." remarks LeDrun from upon

Polisco's nose.

"And look at him," continues Polisco. "Bling-bling fancy plumage and a large breast. Ew, he is fanning out his feathers to impress the fat emperor penguin. I believe the penguin is the chairman of the Committee. You know, whenever someone tries to dazzle you like that, just think about the exposed asshole on the other side. Insurance companies are all parasitic bullshitters. And I wouldn't trust a fanning peacock in a million years. Pass!" Polisco waves his right paw outward into the air.

The scanner moves over to catch the QR code of the emperor penguin.

"Yep. He's the chairman of the committee and a lawyer." Polisco raises his eyebrow while reading the penguin's profile.

"I abhor lawyers. They are all arrogant and crooked money suckers. And look at this fat fruck. Tiny head, tiny legs, and a huge potbelly. His fat could fuel a rocket to a moon and back! I am telling ya, never expect fat frucks to meet deadlines because they won't. They lack something in the blood called discipline." Polisco opines and judges.

"Aren't you a chubby polar..." LeDrun points out from Pol's nose.

"Hey! Mine is genetic, ok?" growls Polisco in defense. "It's not my fault. Anyway, don't use a fat penguin's law firm. The ridiculously expensive legal fees literally feed him. Yet this fat fruck would surely fail to show in court. No way. Next!" Polisco moves his fPhone scanner around the crowd.

The scanner catches a grizzly.

"Ugh, a realtor. She looks like the mother of her airbrushed profile picture." The mean polar bear remarks while checking the grizzly's profile page on his fPhone. "Realtors are the worst snobbish animals ever. Sure. Rich animals like Hiporno are pretentious snobs because more money gives them the illusion that they are better. But realtors are not even rich!"

"You'd better go interact with someone. Anyone! I sense impending trouble," warns and urges LeDrun.

"Oh! She's from Moon Sawa!" Polisco totally ignores the pimple on his nose. "Moon Sawa has the evilest government in the entire universe! I wouldn't trust anyone from that place. What if she's a spy?"

Polisco leans against the hay bale and goes on and on as the scanner catches one animal after another:

"A beaver landscaper. I loathe beavers. They are rodents! Look at his two large shiny front teeth. He can probably gnaw down my entire backyard in one night. Pass."

"A buffalo construction contractor. I detest all horny animals: bucks, rhinos, elk… They just love to swank their hardness on their heads. Losers."

"A car sales doe? What do does know about cars?!"

As Polisco is immersed in his scanning and filtering game, two buff longhorn oxen approach him.

"Sir," says one of the oxen. "We received a warning from the reception desk that a red-nosed polar bear is acting suspiciously. We've watched you for a while and are now convinced that you are not mentally well, given that you have been standing here all alone talking to yourself the whole time. Which hospital do you receive your treatments, or you self-quarantine? We can drop you off." The security oxen grab Polisco's arms and escort him out.

"Wait! I am not a lunatic!" shouts Polisco on his way out. "This is outrageous! I am gonna sue your ass off and have this entire place shut down!"

As they pass the entrance, Pilferine's face acts shocked, while her eyes laugh out loud: "Why are you leaving so soon? Time for your pills already?"

Polisco roars while the red pimple cannot help but guffaw from upon the bear's nose.

"Did you hear that? I told you he's a coocoo," one longhorn ox moos to the other.

# 30

## Privileged Quarantine

Polisco is too pissed to talk on his way home. As he enters the neighborhood, the polar bear notices that all the trashcans are still lined up along the street, waiting to be emptied out. An evil smile leaks out through the corner of his mouth. The good neighbor drives past his garage, slams on the gas, and knocks Pilferine's trashcan down on the ground. The trashcan's lid is forced open like a beached fish with a wide-open mouth, gushing out all sorts of rotten rancid garbage from the dark inside.

"I'm home!" announces Polisco as he opens the door like a champion.

"Master Pol! You came back so soon! How did it go? Did you meet any interesting business animals? I want to hear all about it! Why is your nose so red?" BarKockalotte dashes over to the doorway, wagging his tail like a windshield wiper in a storm.

"How about some selfies with famous animals in town? Can I have them and replace your face with mine?" meows Purrplexy from behind the dog.

"Whoa! Where is the sleigh?" teases PanRoo from the couch in the living room.

"Rude off!" squeals Joecub in his mom's arms.

"Ah hahaha! It's me!" LeDrun appears in the air, convulsed with laughter.

The death messenger flies to the sunroom and summons the family:

"Come together. I will tell you what happened to him in the barnyard."

"No. You won't!" warns the polar bear in vain.

***********

In the sunroom, LeDrun sits on the edge of the windowsill with legs dangling around. Polisco slouches into one of the swivel chairs. He crosses his arms over his chest, ready to defend himself. PanRoo in the other chair exhibits a hue of excitement about the gossip that she's about to hear. The pets and the cub line up on the floor under the windowsill, facing up towards the storyteller like three blooming flowers.

"They kicked him out of the barnyard," says LeDrun, smiling at the scowling polar bear.

"What did you do?" PanRoo yells at Polisco.

"Nothing," Polisco shrugs. "I was doing background checking. All of a sudden, two longhorn oxen showed up and dragged me out of the barnyard. Unbelievable!"

"What background checking?" woofs BarKockalotte out of curiosity.

"Species, professions, genders, colors, looks… you know, the usual stuff." Polisco casually lists off his background check criteria.

"Did you see any town celebrities or hot tomcats by any chance?" chatters Purrplexy at the polar bear.

"No. He didn't talk to anyone." LeDrun shakes his head.

"Honestly, I'm not surprised," sneers PanRoo. "You have borderline zoophobia, specism, sexism, xenophobia, homo…"

"Gee, what do you really think, a woman of color from a third world moon?" Polisco retaliates at Pan's ruthless accusation.

"You called me what?!" roars PanRoo as she suddenly stands up and glares at Polisco.

*Love in the knowing*

*Fear in the know*

*Ongoing exploration*

*Instant recognition*

LeDrun chants while pursing his wrinkly lips to blow out the flaring anger in the bear couple's eyes.

"You said that earlier this morning. It doesn't quite make sense," barks BarKockalotte.

"Knowing yourself and others through Love is an ongoing exploration of the Essence. It flourishes in the present as it engages in dynamic interplay between your Love-charged Energy and others'. Think about things you are passionate about: you enjoy the experience of doing it; think about those you love in life: you enjoy spending time with them. You never stop your ongoing exploration of them as they are always growing and full of changes," illuminates LeDrun.

"Right," rebukes PanRoo with lingering anger. "Polisco stopped learning about me ever since we got married!"

"I'm fully aware of all your changes like your growing bad tempter and clothing size!" Polisco fires back.

"Sh…sh," LeDrun shushes the couple. "On the other hand, perceiving the world through Fear requires instant recognition of risks and potential danger in order to take safety precautions. It relies on the information you've gathered in the past to predict the future. That

'Fear in the know' indicates how Fear, the intrinsic Guard, charges your Energy to recognize, distinguish, analyze and often predict risks. It is a screening and filtering process that aims to avoid dangerous encounters. For knowing the world:

*Love is curious*

*Fear is wary*

*Love experiences*

*Fear identifies*

*Love explores*

*Fear evaluates*

*Love appreciates uniqueness*

*Fear distinguishes differences*

*Love creates*

*Fear predicts*

*Love poses questions*

*Fear collects answers*

*Love immerses in the present*

*Fear values pasts and futures*

*Love updates*

*Fear reinforces*

*Love in the knowing*

*Fear in the know"*

***********

"I did just that at the barnyard!" defenses Polisco. "I just wanted to know something about the participants first. I'm gonna K-I-L-L Pilferine!"

The ousted polar bear grits his teeth and clenches his paws.

"I was on your nose." LeDrun shakes his head like a pellet drum.

"Knowing others through either Love Energy or Fear Energy requires Energy exchange, which is how the Universal Language communicates. When you receive each other's Energy, you intuitively know if it's Love-charged or Fear-charged. Remember the horned viper you encountered in the desert? And how you communicated with each other through Energy exchange?"

"Oh, yeah," recollects Polisco. "I almost stepped on the mother snake's baby eggs."

"That's how Fear protects you," elucidates LeDrun. "However, at the barnyard, you didn't exchange your Energy with any animals except Pilferine. You quickly judged everyone and filtered out all of them. That is highly unnatural. I believe your Fear is somehow manipulated by an outside force."

"No. It's not! It's my freewill!" denies Polisco.

"Ok. But how do you really know anyone without essential communication? Through their profiles on your fPhone or the colors of their fur?" questions the death messenger. "Those are no more than a shape of a tortoise, a buzzing fly or a pimple on the nose: merely exhibited manifestations. Meanwhile, since there was no Energy exchange between you and most of the barnyard animals, your Fear didn't perceive or interpret signals sent from others either. However, your Fear did in fact charge your Energy to repel those animals. That's how I know that you are infected. Because:

### Love in the knowing
### Fear in the know
### The Virus meddles in the middle

"Welcome to the 'V' club, master Pol!" howls BarKockalotte.

PanRoo and Purrplexy growl and yowl upon the realization that

Polisco is infected as well.

The cub squeals and claps his tiny paws with confusion.

"I don't have the Virus! I'm invincible! It's all bunk!" Polisco's roars and protests are engulfed in the family's disturbing commotion.

# 31

## In the Cloud

Late at night, the family is sound asleep. A bear paw creeps into PanRoo's pouch and robs away the snoring tortoise.

"What do you think you are doing?" yells LeDrun while Polisco sneaks out of the bedroom.

"Shush," whispers the polar bear. "Could we go to your secret place in the clouds and conquer the Virus in me before the family wakes up? Then I can still claim that I'm invincible."

"Close your eyes and put your least-filthy paw on my chest button," yawns LeDrun. "But if we fail, the whole family will join us at dawn."

***********

Joecub wakes up in the clouds. White waves ebb and flow toward the horizon, riding through beams of morning glory to buoy up the bright orange fireball. The cub is cuddled by numerous soft white foam balls. He trudges around, laughing and squeaking like in a ball pit. Hungry and exploratory, the bear cub carefully cups a tiny ball of cloud with both paws and puts it in his mouth. Like a swimming marshmallow, the ball of cloud instantly disappears on his tongue without a trace.

"Mr. Bar!" Joecub pushes the dog next to him as he snorts and drools. "Gone!"

"What gone?" BarKockalotte's eyes are forced wide open on the dazed dogface.

"Arf-arf! My holy bone! Where is our bed? Where are we? Master Pan! Master Pol! We have been abducted!" barks BarKockalotte, wide-awake and deeply panicked upon the realization of the strange situation.

"Quiet!" yowls Purrplexy next to the dog. Eyes closed, she curls up into a ball of fur and covers her flattened ears with both paws.

"What's going on?" yawns PanRoo, sitting up and inquiring.

"Master Pan, master Pol is gone!" BarKockalotte reports to the matriarch.

"What do you mean?" PanRoo looks around in pretended calmness.

"Polisco! Master Pol! Daddy!" the family searches for the missing polar bear among the clouds.

***********

"Over here!" In front of a jellyfish-shaped iridescent cloud, stand Polisco and LeDrun, waving and shouting.

The family trudges and plods through the clouds toward the iridescence.

"Caution your paws while cloud walking! Don't twist your ankles!" LeDrun squeals a friendly reminder.

"Clouds? We are walking on clouds? Oh no! My burns just healed!" Purrplexy recollects her sky diving experience when the Love balloon ejected her at the I Resort. The cat feels that her paws and legs are suddenly enfeebled as if they were melting away into the clouds.

"We are walking on clouds? Oh no! My acrophobia!" BarKockalotte cannot feel his legs.

"Oh, boy!" mutters LeDrun. He then raises his voice and shouts at the fear-frozen pets:

"Close your eyes and imagine that you are ice skating!"

Purrplexy and BarKockalotte sit as still as sculptures.

LeDrun shakes his head and fans his turkey neck. The tortoise ponders for a while and then whirls his right arm in a circle as if he were holding a very long lasso and aiming to noose the cat.

Slowly, Purrplexy slides forward as LeDrun reels in the invisible leash.

"I do that to the dog when he refuses to go home from the park," remarks Polisco, arms crossed.

"I'll just hold on to the cat," woofs BarKockalotte. He seizes the free ride opportunity and latches his paws onto the cat's tail.

Joecub follows suit and links his tiny bear paws to the dog's tail.

PanRoo holds her cub as the caboose of the animal train.

"You guys cannot be serious! Help! Police!" groans and grunts the tortoise while pulling, veins popping out.

***********

The animal train arrives at an iridescent cloud gate. Passing through a winding ice tunnel, they enter into a snow hut. Inside the hut erects a giant pyramid of glassy shards from the center of the floor to the ceiling of the hut.

LeDrun guzzles from his crystal flask to recharge from the earlier locomotive work.

"Hey!" Polisco greets the family with excitement. "Don't you just love igloos? The temperature AND shape!"

"So, this is your secret place? What do you need us for? A White Christmas party? Where is the evidence you've collected?" PanRoo gets to work immediately.

"Yes," burps the death messenger. "See the mound of shards?" LeDrun points at the floor-to-ceiling jagged heap. "I have a hypothesis for what they are, but I need your help to prove it. Polisco begged me to take him here last night. But he couldn't resist playing with the snow like a frenzied giant cub, so he just fell asleep snoring like a boom car. Completely useless."

"Hey! I'm a polar bear deprived of snow! And for the record, I did suggest that I pee on the pile. You vetoed it. It's not my fault!" argues Polisco.

"I don't like this place. It's too cold and too high in the sky. I'm out of here!" yowls Purrplexy.

As BarKockalotte attempts to press the running cat down on the icy floor, the pyramid of clear shards suddenly gives off a transient purple glitter, like a death signal from LeDrun's Lair.

"Did you see that flash of purple? That's why you are all here." A mysterious smile leaks from the corner of the death messenger's mouth.

# 32

## Monster in the Middle

The death messenger lays his eyes on Purrplexy on the icy floor. The cat curls up into a ball of fur with one paw covering her closed eyes to block out the bizarre happenings around her. LeDrun wipes off a smirk on his wrinkly face and opens his arms to the oblivious cat. With his raised arms, the magic tortoise levitates Purrplexy in mid-air.

"Open your eyes, Lexy. We are home." The death messenger blatantly lies to the cat.

Purrplexy opens her eyes, only to find out that she is in mid-air all by herself, spectated by the family as well as the mischievous death messenger.

"What the fruck? Put me down! I'm gonna die!" The cat screams as she wriggles in the air.

Like a charm, the crystal chards pyramid, again, flickers purple.

The death messenger nods his head with satisfaction as if he has solved a puzzle.

"What's going on? Why are you torturing the cat? Why exactly are we all here?" frowns PanRoo, grabbing the levitating cat into her arms.

"It's a long story," narrates LeDrun. "A while ago, the Nature Law Office launched an internal investigation on the Death department. They claimed that we've missed tons of death cases on Planet **F**. It is unprecedented and unfathomable because all we death messengers do is follow Nature's design. And Nature never fails. Anywho, the investigation didn't interest other death messengers a bit, but deeply triggered my curiosity, thanks to PaGoo for indulging me with this." The death messenger flashes his crystal flask.

"What's inside your flask anyway?" woofs BarKockalotte, tilting his dog head.

"Pee! Pee!" squeals Joecub as if he knew the answer.

"Could you take care of him, Mr. Bar?" asks PanRoo.

"Fine..." The pouty dog reluctantly takes the bear cub to the other side of the shards mound to urinate.

***********

"So, I began my own secret investigation into the Planet **F** case," continues LeDrun. "I flew around the globe and saw shards everywhere, glittering in purple. I knew that purple when I saw it--it carries death signals. What puzzled me was why it did not come from real lives, but from crystal shards. So, I started to collect them and hide them in this snow hut. It's my vacation igloo for a fling...umm, recreation."

"How did you end up at Pilferine's then?" growls Polisco.

LeDrun sighs deeply: "One day at my lair, I was contemplating the mystery of these glittery shards all over Planet **F**. As I gazed at the purple death signals that were striking the roof, a crazy idea crawled into my mind. I decided to trace one of these premature death signals that contained an embedded signal asking for help. I thought maybe I could find some answers."

"What's a premature signal? Like PE?" meows Purrplexy the wild cat.

"I was a champion of PE in school!" howls the dog from the other side of the chard mound.

"Hey buddy, I don't think she meant physical education!" shouts the polar bear to the innocent dog.

"Quiet!" reproves LeDrun. "A premature death signal indicates the faint idea of death, but not actual death. Death messengers follow Nature's design: we are only meant to be summoned AFTER an actual death, but never BEFORE it. My curiosity and my desire to help, however, were so strong that I decided to precede our natural summoning by tracing a premature death signal. So, I randomly picked one among millions of them and traced it back to Pilferine's house, whence I saw the Virus for the first time."

"A-aaaa!" The fluffy animals scream.

The shard pyramid flashes purple light again.

"What does the monster look like?" asks PanRoo, holding the cat in her arms tightly.

"It was all dark and blurry." LeDrun recollects the traumatic memories. "I saw the poor boar raccoon. His Fear bubble appeared hard, like fortified glass. His mouth was propped wide open from the inside, out of which squirmed out a purple monster. It had a worm shaped body and a round, spiky head."

"So the Virus looks like a purple penis." Polisco imparts his wisdom.

"The monster shattered the fortified-glass-like Fear bubble into pieces," LeDrun continues, leering at the polar bear. "The Virus wrapped its body around the raccoon and whispered something to his ear. As if he were possessed or hypnotized, the poor animal went straight to the safe, took a gun out, put it in his mouth and pulled the trigger. Zero hesitation."

"You didn't try to save him?" PanRoo asks a rhetorical question.

"I didn't know how," frowns LeDrun. "And it all happened so fast. The raccoon's death felt like the receptor button on my chest had exploded like a nuclear bomb. I felt extreme pain and lost consciousness. The next thing I saw was the inside of Pan's pouch."

"So curiosity didn't just kill the cat," mocks Purrplexy, feeling safe again in Pan's arms.

"Real funny, kitten." The tortoise gives the cat a quick glance. "As I was living in your house and healing, I meditated profoundly under the maple tree as well as on the windowsill. I believe that Nature has designed the way that we death messengers can only collect the Essence AFTER life ends in order to protect us. Every signal has its proper channel to reach the receptor. Our natural summoning is to wait for our receptor to be struck by an actual death signal. I shouldn't have messed with it. It's the price I had to pay for disrespecting Nature's design. More importantly, I've come up with a hypothesis. I believe that the crystal shards I've collected on Planet **F** are ruptured pieces of every victim's Fear bubble, within which the Virus has lived to feed off the hosts' Fear Energy."

Silence.

***********

"No one remains perpetually in Fear. If your theory were right, the Virus would've starved to death because it opts out of the host's Love Energy." Polisco challenges after contemplation.

"I think I know why the Virus preys on Fear," articulates LeDrun.

"***Love attracts then bonds; Fear repels then distances.*** If you were the Virus, would you prey on a closely interconnected animal, or pounce on an isolated one? And regarding how the Virus keeps the host in constant Fear, I have no answer but a suspicion that the Virus has a malicious trick that alters how the host perceives the world, as well as how it communicates with others. This causes their Fear bubble to be inflating all the time, such that the more Fear Energy the Virus gets, the faster it grows. The moment it becomes fully-grown, it bursts out of the Fear bubble for independence and propagation. Simultaneously, it kills the host and absorbs the ultimate Fear Energy that's supposed to send the death signal to the universe. I believe this could explain why we've missed so many death cases on Planet **F**."

"You mean like the Monster-in-the-middle? We call it MITM in information security," ponders Polisco, the cyber security engineer.

"Do explain!" The death messenger is intrigued.

"Ahem!" Polisco clears his throat for shoptalk. "The **monster-in-the-middle** is an attacker that sneaks in between the communication of two parties. It could actually alter the message in-between for its own benefit, and yet make both parties believe that they are engaged in direction communication. A successful MITM is an excellent impersonator…"

"N…er…d…" Purrplexy encrypts the letters in a broadcast yawn. "So the Virus somehow creeps into the victim's Fear bubble and makes the sucker believe that it's legit and trustworthy? How?"

"And how exactly does the Virus intercept the messages from outside, and then alter them into something that incites the victim to act upon their Fear?" PanRoo gangs up on Polisco.

The cornered polar bear roars: "I don't know! Ask LeDrunk! It's like the **monster-in-the-middle**, the MITM attack!"

# 33

## The Virus Code

BarKockalotte's ears are up the whole time, listening from the other side of the chard pyramid. Overhearing his master Pol's analysis of the Virus' evil trick, the canine eavesdropper has a spark of enlightenment in his eyes. The dog struts towards the gang and woofs: "According to master Pol, the Virus may have a secret code, an argot, a parlance, you know, a programming language."

"The Virus Code?" wonders and ponders Polisco.

PanRoo, however, notices something of more importance than the Virus Code.

"Where is Joecub?" The concerned mother asks the babysitting dog.

"He…umm…is definitely somewhere," stutters BarKockalotte.

Suddenly, the bear cub's painful screeches from the other side of the shard pyramid hurt the animals' ears.

The shards sparkle in bright deathly purple.

***********

PanRoo throws the cat onto the icy floor and hops away to check on the cub. Polisco and LeDrun follow.

"Son of a meowtch!" The cat victim yowls and swears as she hits the floor. She picks herself up with a pouty face and joins the gang.

Joecub sits at the foot of the shard pyramid base, crying at the sight of his bleeding paw.

"Mr. Bar!" PanRoo yells at the designated babysitter.

"I'm a police dog, not a nanny..." whines and mumbles BarKockalotte.

"Jo's cry is a perfect reminder," smiles LeDrun. "The reason I've gathered you all here is because I need your collective Fear Energy to test out my hypothesis. You see. I collected these shards on Planet F because they glittered in the purple that signifies death, and Fear Energy is the designated carrier of death signals. But, whenever I bring shards to this secret place in the clouds, they suddenly stop glittering. I suspect it is due to the fact that there is no Fear Energy to re-energize the shards in this pristine igloo. Last night, I took Police here first with all good intentions to stimulate his Fear Energy. Seeing how happy this polar bear was with ice and snow, I simply couldn't incite him. So, enough said. I was wondering if you could stimulate each other's Fear Energy and make it last for a while to prove my hypothesis. It's for pure research. What do you think?" The death messenger rubs his claws with anticipation.

"You are wasting your time, LeDrunk. I have no Fear Energy to offer," claims Polisco, puffing up with pride.

"Let me try!" PanRoo takes the challenge. She roars at Pol: "Male polar bears' size is not the biggest in the world! There are black bears, grizzly bears, hippo..."

"I don't understand what you are saying because of your thick accent!" Polisco retaliates.

"I love this game!" howls BarKockalotte. He scuffs the acrophobic cat and lifts her all the way up in the air like a canine Statue of Liberty holding a feline torch in the right paw.

"Put me down, Uggo! The masters love me more!" The cat kicks and screams from up in the air.

The couple is fighting; the pets are brawling; the cub is crying. The pile of shards glares out like a pyramid of purple fireworks. The tortoise grins and levitates above the whole scene, like a shinning star hung upon the highest bough.

***********

Strangely, the shards start to separate from the pile. They begin to float around and form a circle as if they were searching for something. One after another, the Fear bubble pieces reshuffle and then aggregate into a purple crystal sphere in resemblance of the globe of Planet **F**.

"Something's written on the inner surface of the ball!" barks BarKockalotte.

"It's hardly intelligible because it's reversed and inverted," meows Purrplexy.

"I think I see the word '**cat**,'" PanRoo discerns.

"You are the Virus!" barks BarKockalotte at Purrplexy.

"It's '**cat ego**,' idiot!" The cat hisses at the dog.

"**Cat…ego…rize, categorize!**" LeDrun puts the first puzzle together.

"'**Ass**' is next to it," Polisco detects with his expertise.

"**Assify**!" adds BarKockalotte, howling with excitement.

"Good Lord. What's '**assify**'? Make you an ass? But you already are," Purrplexy jeers at the dog.

"I think it's **classify**." PanRoo announces her verdict.

"I discern the word '**polar**,' but that can't be master Pol. It must be my eyes…" BarKockalotte whines with self-doubt, wagging his tail at Polisco the polar bear.

"Cold!" coos Joecub in Pan's arms while blowing on his tiny bear paws.

"The Virus Code!" The family shouts in stereo.

"We got it. Great teamwork!" acclaims LeDrun. "As soon as we decipher the Virus Code, we can reverse engineer its attack mechanism and beat the Virus."

***********

During the animals' exultant celebration of the breakthrough, the icy floor and the snow walls suddenly begin shaking like a violent earthquake. Huge seismic waves surge across the clouds as if an army were marching toward them.

"Avalanche!" The family storms out of the snow hut.

On the clouds trudges PaGoo, the life messenger. She bellows with anger at the sight of the family:

"The Life Lab is infected with the Virus. And you are all to blame."

TO BE CONTINUED